HARVEST IN TRANSLATION

Also by Pawel Huelle

Who Was David Weiser?

Pawel Huelle

Moving House

Stories

■ ■ ■

Translated by

Michael Kandel

A Harvest Book
A Helen and Kurt Wolff Book
Harcourt Brace & Company
San Diego   New York   London

Copyright © 1991 by Pawel Huelle
Revised English translation copyright © 1995
by Harcourt Brace & Company

This is a translation of *Opowiadania na czas przeprowadzki*.

Library of Congress Cataloging-in-Publication Data
Huelle, Paweł, 1957–
[Short stories. English. Selections]
Moving house and other stories / Paweł Huelle: translated from
the Polish.—1st ed.
p.   cm.
"A Helen and Kurt Wolff book."
Contents: The table—Snails, puddles, rain—Moving house—
Uncle Henryk—A miracle—In Dublin's fair city—Mina.
ISBN 0-15-162731-2
ISBN 0-15-600251-5 (pbk.)
1. Huelle, Paweł, 1957–   —Translations into English.   I. Title.
PG7167.U86A25   1994
891.8'537—dc20   93-48587

The text was set in Joanna.
Designed by Kaelin Chappell
Printed in the United States of America
First Harvest edition 1996

A   B   C   D   E

Contents

The Table

■ ■ ■

I

"Oh, that table!" my mother would shriek. "I just can't stand it any more! Other people have decent furniture. We're the only ones with a thing like that." She'd point at the round table where we ate our dinner every day. "Can you really call that a table?" she'd ask, her voice faltering and her shoulders drooping.

My father wouldn't rise to her goading; he'd withdraw into himself, and the room would fill with a heavy silence. Actually, the table wasn't all that bad. Its one shorter leg was propped up with a wedge, and its scarred surface could be covered with a tablecloth. My father had bought the table from Mr. Polaske of Zaspa in 1946, when Mr. Polaske packed his bags and took the last train west to Germany. In exchange, my father gave Mr. Polaske a pair of army boots a Soviet sergeant had swapped him for a secondhand watch, and since the boots were not in mint condition, my father threw in some butter from UNRRA. Moved

by this gesture, Mr. Polaske gave my father, in
addition to the table, a photograph from his family album. It showed two elegant men in suits,
standing on Lange Brücke. I liked to look at this
photograph, not out of interest in Mr. Polaske and
his brother, of whom I knew very little, but because in the background stretched a view that I'd
sought in vain on Long Harbor. Dozens of fishing
boats were moored at the Fish Market quay, the
jetty was crowded with people buying and sell-
ing, and barges and steamships were sailing by
on the Motława river, their funnels as tall as
masts. The place was full of bustle and life, Lange
Brücke looked like a real port, and although the
signs above hotels, bars, and counting houses
looked foreign, it was an attractive scene anyway.
In no way did it resemble Long Harbor, which
indeed was rebuilt after the great fire and bombardment, but which was a wasteland of offices
of no use to anyone, of red slogans hanging on
walls, and the green thread of the Motława,
where a militia motor boat sputtered up and
down and once a day the Border Guard's ship
went by.

"It's a German table," my mother would say,
raising her voice. "You should have hacked it to
bits years ago. When I think," she'd go on, a little
calmer now, "that a Gestapo man used to sit at it
and eat his eels after work, it makes me sick."

My father would shrug and hold out the photograph of Mr. Polaske.

"Look," he'd say to my mother, "is that a Gestapo man?" Then he'd tell the story of Mr. Polaske, who was a Social Democrat and spent three years in the Stutthof concentration camp because he didn't agree with Hitler. When our city was incorporated into the Reich in 1939, Mr. Polaske ostentatiously did not hang a flag out on his house, and after that they took him away.

"Well, then his brother was a Gestapo man." My mother would cut the discussion short and go into the kitchen, while my father, upset by the loss of half his audience, would tell the story of the other Mr. Polaske, who immediately after the war had gone to Warsaw with Senator Kunze to ask President Bierut to allow the Gdańsk Germans to stay if they sign a declaration of loyalty.

"Then," my father's tale went on, "President Bierut twisted his moustache, and told the delegates that the German Social Democrats had never erred on the side of sound historical judgement, and that they had long since betrayed their class instinct, of which Comrade Stalin had written so wisely and comprehensively. Any kind of request—President Bierut clenched his worker's fist and hit the desk—is an anti-government act." Then Mr. Polaske's brother returned to Gdańsk and hanged himself in the attic of their home in Zaspa. And why do you think he did that?" my father would ask loudly. "After all, he could have gone back to Germany like his brother."

"He hanged himself," my mother would say as she came into the room with a steaming dish, "because he was finally troubled by his conscience. If all Germans were troubled by their conscience, they'd all do the same," she'd add as she set the potatoes in jackets on the table. "They should all hang themselves, after what they've done."

"And the Soviets?" my father would exclaim, shoving potato skins to the edge of his plate, "what about the Soviets?"

I knew that a quarrel would start immediately. My mother had a great fear of Germans, and nothing could possibly cure her of that fear, whereas my father reserved his greatest grudge for the compatriots of Fyodor Dostoyevsky. An invisible border now ran across Mr. Polaske's table, splitting my parents apart, just as in 1939, when the land of their childhood, scented with apples, halva, and a wooden pencil-case with crayons rattling in it, was ripped in half like a piece of canvas, with the silver thread of the river Bug glittering down the middle.

"I saw them," my father would say, as he gulped white pieces of potato, "I saw them . . ."

What he meant, of course, was the parade in the little town where the two armies met. "They raised the dust to the very heavens," my father would say, helping himself to more crackling, "and they marched abreast in step, and they sang now in German, now in Russian, but the Russian was louder, because the Soviets had sent a whole regiment to the parade—the Germans only sent two companies."

"The Germans were worse," my mother would interrupt, "they had no human feelings."

I didn't like these conversations, especially not when they got underway over dinner, and the strong flavor of broth or the fragrant aroma of horseradish sauce was infused with the thunder of cannon-fire or the clatter of a train carrying people off to a slow or instant death. I didn't like it when they argued about such things, because they forgot about me, and there I was, stuck between them, like a used and useless object. The one to blame for it all was Mr. Polaske. And his table. That's what I used to think, as I forced down my jacket potatoes or cheese pierog. If it weren't for Mr. Polaske and his table, my parents would be chatting about a Marilyn Monroe film or this year's strawberry crop, or about the latest launching at the Lenin shipyard, which Premier Cyrankiewicz had attended. As time passed, Mr. Polaske's table became more and more like a bad tooth. Whenever the pain grew weaker and seemed to have passed, they'd be seized by an irresistible urge to touch the sore spot and start the throbbing agony again.

Was there anything I could have done? If the problem had been a chair, I'd certainly have coped. But the oak table was so large, round and heavy, with those carved legs—too massive for me to destroy without anyone's help. I began to suspect that Mr. Polaske had left it to us on purpose, that he knew about the invisible border that ran between my parents and had felt sure his piece of furniture, which he couldn't take with him to Germany, would be the cause of constant argument. My father, not liking change, stuck to his guns, and my mother burned the bigos or the spareribs more and more often, and continually found new shortcomings in the German table. Then, in addition to its lame leg and blistered veneer, came woodworm, whose clandestine work, though inaudible by day, kept my mother up at night. In the morning she'd be tired and bad-tempered.

"Do something," she'd say to my father. "I can't stand it any longer! Those are German worms. Soon they'll attack the dresser and the cupboard, because they are insatiable, like everything German," she'd whisper in his ear.

If Mr. Polaske had wanted to avenge himself, he couldn't have found a better way. Often I imagined him rubbing his hands together and laughing to himself somewhere in Hamburg or Munich. He'd have eaten the butter from UNRRA in a matter of days, and worn out the Soviet boots after a year or so, yet we were still suffering with his table. It was like a boarder who's always getting in everybody's way but impossible to kick out. Why should he want revenge on us? I sometimes wondered. We'd done him no harm. We weren't even living in his house, which was now occupied by some high Party official. Could he have wished us ill simply because we were Polish? I could find no ready answer to that question, nor indeed to any question that concerned Mr. Polaske. For hours I'd gaze at the photograph in which Long Harbor looked like a real port; I'd count the funnels of the steamships winding their way along the Motława. Meanwhile, with each day that passed, the table seemed larger, swelling to impossible dimensions within the cramped room.

At last one day the inevitable happened. As my mother set down a tureen full of soup, the wedge came loose under the short leg and the table staggered like a wounded animal. Beet soup splashed on my father's shirt and trousers.

"Oh!" cried my mother with delight, clapping her hands together. "Didn't I tell you this would happen?"

My father said not a word. He replaced the wedge, ate his second course, and waited for the cherry blancmange in silence. It was only after dessert, that he went down to the cellar, a cigarette between his teeth, to get his saw and tape-measure. Soon he was leaning over the table, squinting with one eye, then the other, impressive as a battlefield surgeon about to operate. But what happened next was amazing. My father, so handy at repairs, couldn't fix Mr. Polaske's table, or, rather, couldn't fix it's uneven legs. After each cut, it would turn out that one of the legs was a little shorter than the others. Possessed by the fury of perfection, or maybe the fury of German methodicalness, my father refused to admit defeat: he shortened and shortened the legs, until at last an extraordinary sight presented itself. On the floor, beside heaps of sawn-off bits of wood and a sea of sawdust, lay the top of Mr. Polaske's table, legless, like a great brown shield. My mother's eyes glittered with emotion, my father's look was black as thunder, but nothing could stop him from finishing what he had begun. The snarling saw began to rip into the tabletop. My father puffed and panted, and my mother held her breath, until at last she cried: "Well, finally!"

Mr. Polaske's table was only good for burning now.

My father took the bits of wood down to the cellar, my mother swept up the sawdust, but I had a feeling in my bones that this wasn't the end of the matter, that the real trouble was yet to come.

The next day we ate dinner in the kitchen. It was cramped and uncomfortable, and the smell of fried herring, thick as a cloud, did nothing to help my appetite.

"We'll have to buy a new table," said my mother, "a little smaller than the old one, perhaps, but it should be round as well. And then some new chairs," she said, dreamily, "with plush covers!"

My father remained silent. After dinner we took the tram to the furniture shop. The salesman threw his arms wide in a gesture of helplessness, smiled knowingly, and said that what he had was what we saw: triangular tables.

"It's the latest model," he said, pointing to an equilateral object. "Experimental."

"And round ones?" asked my mother. "Aren't there any round ones?"

The salesman explained that this year's central plan had already been fulfilled, and that there would be some round tables, of course there would be, but not until January or February. My father gave an acid smile; it was the middle of May. My mother, meanwhile, walked among the triangular tables, touching their surfaces, as if in disbelief and horror. Light streamed into the shop through the dusty window, illuminating her chestnut hair with a discreet halo that gave her a melancholy air.

Once we were outside, she said we should try another shop. What a disappointment she was in for! Over all the furniture shops in town hovered the central plan like one of the Fates. The only non-triangular table anywhere, brought out at her insistence from a murky storeroom, was rectangular, very long and narrow and utterly unsuitable for our room. I didn't know if Mr. Polaske could have foreseen this. After a few hours' fruitless search, we came home exhausted, his table sticking in us like a barely visible splinter.

"Well," my father said, "we can always order a table. It'll be more expensive, but"—here he paused meaningfully and raised a finger like a preacher—"in view of the central plan we have no other choice."

What could be simpler than such reasoning? Nothing could, and yet, as it soon turned out, of the five carpenters' workshops in the neighborhood three had closed down long ago. Their owners, ruined by taxes, now worked at the state factory, fulfilling the central plan. The fourth, which belonged to a Mrs. Rupiejek, the widow of a carpenter from Wilno, was going out of business. The fifth workshop had become a quiet little company dedicated exclusively to making beautiful coffins, which were exempt—at least so far—from central planning.

"Everything in its own time," said my father on his return from town. "They too will be sucked into the stream of history."

But we still had no table. My father made several timid, poetic improvisations that were doomed to failure at their very inception. He balanced the ironing board on twin chests; he knocked together a provisional table-top in the cellar; he decided to place an advertisement in the morning paper—"Wanted: secondhand table. If round, I'll buy." None of this found favor in my mother's eyes. The advertisement seemed to her particularly dreadful. We'd already had a second-hand table, and look what happened! Our final hope lay with Mr. Gorzki, who with no shop sign or permit, official or unofficial, did a bit of carpentry on the side. He did it after working hours, using materials pilfered from the shipyard. Moreover, he asked for large deposits and drank every Saturday and Sunday as if he were a sailor and not a carpenter. Mr. Gorzki often slept on a rickety bench in front of his house, and that happened on Sundays, the people coming back from church would point their fingers at him and call him a Freemason. Anyway, he took a large deposit from my father and promised to make a table within a week. A table and as round as they come. My mother was very pleased, but my father, who was law-abiding, fretted all that week.

"If I know," he'd ask loudly each evening, "that he's making us a table out of stolen wood, isn't that wrong? Dishonest?"

But my mother was a pragmatist.

"Who's it stealing from? Everything belongs to the state. Everything!" she said, making a big circle in the air with her arm, as if the Spirit of History were speaking through her.

The Spirit spoke with even more authority through Mr. Gorzki. The carpenter did not complete his drinking on Sunday evening, but prolonged his state of bliss through Monday. He resumed it on Tuesday, sustained it on Wednesday, and expertly added impetus on Thursday, until he'd pulled through to Friday after midnight, Saturday and Sunday lay ready and waiting for him in thirsty anticipation. On Monday, my father and I arrived at Mr. Gorzki's shed, which stood next to the pond behind the brewery, where he received us sitting on the dirt floor, dead drunk, amid a sea of bottles and scattered tools. His face shone with a mixture of gloom and ecstasy. Now and then he raised his head, guffawed throatily and croaked out the same sentence over and over, like an accordion: "I know! I know!"

My father went purple.

"Where's my money?" he shouted. "Where's our table? Give me back my deposit!" His voice cracked. "Give it back this instant!"

But even I could see that my father's shouting was purely for the sake of appearances. It no longer had anything to do with Mr. Gorzki, who right before our eyes was cutting the threads that tied him to the world of cause and effect.

From then on Mr. Polaske began to make appearances at our apartment. He'd knock very gently at the door, greet my father with a nod, then silently walk around his table, entirely invisible by now. He'd place gifts on it—a package of coffee, some chocolate, a box of English tea—and then he'd slip away quietly, to avoid running into my mother. The presents looked odd hanging in midair, and when I reached out to touch them, they vanished, just like Mr. Polaske, quickly and without trace. The look on my father's face gave me no clue as to which of the brothers it was who came to visit us. Anyway, I never discussed those appearances with my father, who was growing more and more distracted and might not even have noticed the fleeting presence of our guest. The photograph of Long Harbor wasn't much help either. The two Mr. Polaskes were so much alike that I couldn't tell which of them had left for Germany and which had stayed behind for good in the Brętowo cemetery. I was prepared for extraordinary and unlikely things to happen. What, for instance, would be the result of an encounter between my mother and Mr. Polaske? Or an unexpected appearance by our guest at the kitchen table? But nothing like that happened.

One day my father came home from work particularly excited.

"I've got it!" he cried from the doorway. "I've got us a table at last!"

My mother looked out of the window. "I don't see the furniture van," she noted drily.

My father took a slip of paper from his pocket and announced that what we had to do was go to Mr. Kasper, a crafter of tables like the ones before the war—good and solid and round, or oval, or elliptical, whatever the customer desired. And this was the secret of the enterprise: Mr. Kasper accepted commissions only from reliable people, on a personal recommendation. My father flourished the note in the air like a winning lottery ticket, and added that Mr. Kasper the carpenter lived in Żuławy, on the other side of the Vistula.

II

The carpenter's house was like a little wooden box with a small porch and some fancy attic windows, submerged in the greenery of ancient willow trees and shrubs. There we stood in the yard, looking around uncertainly, for there wasn't a living soul about, not even a dog. Eventually a wrinkle-faced woman of indeterminate age came out from the garden which extended behind the house.

"Who is it you want?" she asked.

"Mr. Kasper," said my father, smiling. "We have some business to do with him."

"It's not Kasper, it's Kaspar," said the woman.

"All right," said my father, shifting from foot to foot. "We've got a deal for Mr. Kaspar."

The woman looked at us with suspicion, or maybe just indifference. She didn't say anything else, and we went on standing there in the motionless midday air, like two aliens from another planet.

"We've got something to say to him," my father said at length. "Is he at home?"

"At home?" the woman said indignantly. "You'll have to go down the path 'til you get to the cattle yard. *That's* where he is!" She turned away, the hem of her apron flapping, as if we'd entirely ceased to interest her.

"Come on," my father sighed. "We've got to find him."

Compared with the bus ride over the pontoon bridge across the Vistula or the trip in the open narrow-gauge railway car that had brought us along causeways, canals, and poplar-lined avenues, nimbly leaping across iron bridges and hidden floodgates, the final stage of our expedition in search of a round table was like the road to purgatory. We fought our way across filthy sand, which threw up a thick dust that stung our throats, coated our lips and tongues, made our eyes sting, and felt gritty between our teeth; we were guided by hoofmarks.

"It can't be far now," said my father. "This is the route they drive the cattle along."

But by now I didn't care any more. Even a windmill, as useless as a discarded tool, with stumps for wings, standing next to the path did not attract my attention. The path was covered with animal dung, and we had to be careful not to sink our feet into horse or cow shit. It was blazing hot, and if it hadn't been for my father, I'd have turned back.

At last we reached an open space where a bunker-like building stood. Its square cement walls had no proper windows, only a strip of small skylights running beneath a flat roof. A shabby yellow sign announced that we were standing before the Boar's Head Inn. Inside, it was cool and dingy and several men rather the worse for wear were sitting at wobbly little tables.

"There's no beer left," the portly bartender cried. "They've guzzled it all already."

Swirling trails of tobacco smoke and a strong smell of urine, sweat, and alcohol engulfed us like a mist. My father explained to the bartender who we were looking for, while I scrutinized the customers' faces. They were burnt by the sun and deeply furrowed, all wearing the same expression, one hard to define—as if staring into space.

Mr. Kaspar was sitting in the corner of the bar, almost invisible in the semi-darkness, smoking the stump of a cigar. Instead of an empty beer mug, there was a sheet of paper in front of him, on which he was making violet lines with an indelible pencil. My father took the note out of his pocket, set it down like a visiting card and whispered the story of the table into Mr. Kaspar's ear, drawing lines in the air, cutting them and joining them, rising on tiptoe, then finally sitting down on a bench, while the carpenter listened in silence, smoking the last of his cigar.

Once we'd gone outside, the roles reversed. Dragging along a piglet on a bit of rope, Mr. Kaspar described the day's cattle sale—not a successful one. They were never successful when officials and inspectors came. That was why Mr.

Kaspar hadn't sold his pig, and had sat waiting in the bar for God knows what, for the end of the world, perhaps, or for better days, until he saw us.

We passed the abandoned windmill, and Mr. Kaspar went on talking. He told us that a few days ago he dreamed that a grown man and a little boy came knocking at his door with some good news for him. That premonition had put him in an excellent mood, and it came true today. For what finer thing could happen to a fellow in times like these? My father glanced discreetly at his watch; time was sailing by relentlessly, and the last narrow-gauge train was leaving from the next village in an hour.

"Don't worry," said the carpenter, gripping my father's arm. "What is our life beside eternity? A brief moment, nothing but a speck of dust!"

My father didn't answer, and Mr. Kaspar elaborated his thought further. "Yet in that speck of dust lie hidden destinies. For where are we going? And where have we come from?"

"Yes, indeed," said my father, letting his head droop, "it's all a great mystery. But"—he hesitated for a moment—"will you make the table? It's very important to us."

The carpenter had become entangled in the pig's rope, and did not immediately reply to my father's question. The piglet squealed pitifully as

Mr. Kaspar disentangled the twisted coils, and a dense cloud of dust blew up around us, then slowly settled, swirling in the rays of the afternoon sun.

When we reached the house, the wrinkle-faced woman brought out plates and cutlery, while Mr. Kaspar, as if he hadn't heard my father's question or had forgotten the purpose of our visit, set out some wicker armchairs around a small stone table. Before my father had a chance to say anything, we were sitting down to soup with large golden egg yolks floating in it, and then a joint of meat. Once we'd eaten, Mr. Kaspar brought a jug up from the cellar and filled chunky glasses with juniper beer, dark in color, that had a strong, aromatic fragrance.

"The real art of it," he said, raising his glass to eye level, "relies on not adding too many of the little berries—and on picking them at the right time of day, early in the afternoon, when they've been warmed up by the sun and are giving off their juice."

I watched my father as he took long draughts of the cloudy liquid, and as I watched, his face, ever serious, gradually brightened and took on an unusual shine. And the two gentlemen began to reminisce. My father related how in 1945 he'd paddled across the Vistula to Gdańsk in an old canoe, because he didn't have any documents and

was afraid of railway stations and places fre-
quented by Soviet patrols. Mr. Kaspar spoke of a
long journey by train, which had ended not far
from here when German saboteurs blew up the
tracks. Looking for a place to stay, he'd walked
through empty villages, where he heard the creak
of shutters and doors left ajar softly enticing him:
"Hey, Kaspar, over here! This way, Kaspar, come
here!" But he couldn't make up his mind to stop,
because he'd left the most beautiful city in the
world behind him, a city of churches and syna-
gogues, of gentle hills and pine forests embracing
the suburbs, the city of his childhood, youth, and
war, which was now under Bolshevik power.

"And that's the power of Satan," said Mr. Kaspar pensively. "The land of darkness and cruel
oppression."

By now the jug was empty. The wrinkle-faced
woman took it into the house for a moment.

"But how long is it going to continue?" asked
my father. "How much longer can we put up
with it?"

Mr. Kaspar poured more juniper beer into the
glasses from the refilled vessel. A light evening
mist floated on the air, swallows were swooping
under the eaves, shrilly whistling, and my father,
as if he'd forgotten all about the narrow-gauge
railway and the table, said that the Lord God must

long since have lost interest in us, for a world like this one to be possible.

"Oh, no!" Mr. Kaspar snorted. "We can never be sure what lies ahead. But anyway," he asked, "has the world deserved a better fate?"

After this question, into which like the buzzing of a fly crept doubts and obscure shadows, barely visible and yet plain to see in the form of sudden wrinkles on my father's brow, the leaves began to rustle and a light breeze blew across the garden from the river. Mr. Kaspar had not immediately taken to this land, where the earth is flat as a table and has no end, and long rows of poplars and willows run off in straight lines into infinity. One spring a storm had broken the dams and demolished the floodgates, and the sea had invaded all the way up to here, to the foot of Mr. Kaspar's house.

"Just imagine," he said, leaning toward my father, "I cast my rod out of the window and reeled in a . . . Can you guess?"

"A catfish!" cried my father. "There must be enormous catfish in these canals!"

"It was a fifteen-pound cod!" recalled Mr. Kaspar delightedly. "And after the water had been standing there a while, I could draw in netfuls of herring!"

I coated my palate with the taste of bitter beer,

as I'd been given a couple of mouthfuls to try, and I could feel little juniper bubbles starting to spin in my head. Quietly I left the veranda and sank into the garden undergrowth. I walked along paths thick with burdock, and the strong scent of peonies in the air gave me a foretaste of a hot summer.

"*We're the men of the First Brigade!*" my father's voice soared high above the trees.

"*With a rifle fusillade!*" Mr. Kaspar chimed in, and then they sang in chorus: "*Onto the pyre we cast our lot! Onto the pyre!*"

The two gentlemen let their inebriated voices fly beyond the river Niemen, and after they'd forded it, with a clatter of weapons and a flutter of flags, they drank the health of Marshal Piłsudski, and I heard the smash of breaking glass. Soon after I caught sight of them on a wide lane between apple trees. They were walking slowly toward the river.

"Of course I'll help you. Mind you, I've never done it," my father was saying, "but why not?"

"Yes, yes," the carpenter replied. "I always wait until after dusk, because it's not a simple job. You've got to be careful!"

"Of course, you've got to be very careful," my father repeated like an echo.

The red disk of the moon was rising in the sky as they disappeared into a large shed, closely

planted around with forsythia and hazel. I sat
down nearby at the water's edge and gazed at the
rib cage of a drawbridge. Its drooping arm bi-
sected the river like an immobile crane, and lower
down, among the reeds and rushes, I could see
the wreck of a barge. It had been driven into the
riverbank like a mighty wedge. In the shimmer-
ing moonlight I could see that stunted birch trees
and alders were sprouting on the bow and the
upper part. Not a sound, not even the faintest
splash, broke the silence by the river. The air
stood still, and once again I thought of Mr. Polaske, who had imperceptibly entered our apartment looking for his invisible table. Might he do
it now, while my father and I were at Mr. Kaspar's place by the river Tuja? The last narrow-
gauge train had left hours ago, and by now my
mother was sure to be in the neighbor's apartment calling the police and the hospitals to con-
firm her worst forebodings. What if she were to
pass him, silent and pensive in his long overcoat,
in the dark stairwell? Worse still, what if she saw
him in our apartment?

No sound was coming from the shed, nor was
the faintest ray of light visible through the closed
shutter. It took me a while to notice that a gray
thread of smoke was seeping from a small chim-
ney up into the dark blue sky. I was expecting
the buzz of a saw or the knocking of a hammer

to rip the silence, but instead the air was suddenly pierced by an uncanny scream. Never in my life had I heard anything so terrible. Somewhere between a wail and a squeal, it shattered the air, only to cease abruptly after a few seconds.

I was paralyzed. I stared at the black outline of the shed, as if inside it something had happened between my father and Mr. Kaspar, something that was beyond my ability to imagine. Finally I went to the shed and pushed the door in about an inch. I saw Mr. Kaspar in a white apron splattered with blood. In both hands he raised a cleaver, and I heard my father say loudly, "No, no—not like that!" as it struck something soft that was lying on the table. Blood spurted in all directions, and Mr. Kaspar, wiping red streaks from his face and hands, said, "Yes, maybe it hasn't all flowed out as it should."

A fire was blazing in a large oven that had several little iron doors; my father was tossing logs into the grate, and Mr. Kaspar exchanged the cleaver for a knife and began cutting red and pink hunks from the meat that was hanging on hooks. The head lay nearby on the floorboards. The piglet's eyes gazed at me inquiringly while the two men rinsed the cuts of meat. They put some into earthenware pots, and smeared others with a powder, then hung them on an iron rail that receded into the depths of the tall oven.

"We should be done by morning," said Mr. Kaspar, putting down his long, broad knife. "It's lucky that you came today, because my wife can't bear the sight of anything like this."

My father set aside his work, wiped his hands, and from a crystal decanter that stood on the shelf, he poured a ruby red liquid, thicker and darker than blood, into two glasses.

"Your wife isn't very talkative," said my father, wiping his mouth. "She's got an unusual accent. Pomeranian, but different, somehow."

"You noticed?" said the carpenter, setting to work again.

Before my father had pushed the next gridiron into the oven, Mr. Kaspar began to tell how he dreamed of them at night, how he saw them as clear as day, passing through the entrance to the camps, dressed in those black cloaks of theirs, and going straight to heaven in the same black cloaks, while up above, the Lord God opened the gates and welcomed them with a smile. Who could be dearer to Him than they, who so lovingly tilled the rich land by the sweat of their brows, they, who so industriously dug out canals, built flood-gates, erected windmills, sang psalms and hymns, and would never, not on any account, take up arms?

"They . . . ?" asked my father hesitantly as he set the oven door ajar.

Mr. Kaspar gently sighed and told him about the Mennonites, of whom hardly a trace was left, and about the house he had entered more than a dozen years ago, thinking it was empty like the rest, but there he was mistaken. After two whole days had gone by he saw two eyes shining in the deepest corner of the attic: her eyes, the eyes of a Mennonite, the last in this land and the first he ever saw by the river Tuja.

"Yes," said my father, "now I understand."

The water was bubbling in the pot as the carpenter rinsed off entrails, and over the shed, the garden, the river, and the canals a full moon had risen. I stood in the doorway gazing at the ruby red liquid in the crystal decanter, and the cuts of meat hanging on hooks. After a moment's silence, Mr. Kaspar went on with his story. He had stared into those eyes and knew at once that they understood him, although for long months to come he had been unable to explain to her exactly where he had come from and why he had taken the train so far west. He couldn't describe his city to her, a city set amid hills and pine forests, where the cupolas of churches showed through the clouds, for she knew only one city, the one they used to sail to for the market. It was completely different, and then it was burned down and ruined.

"All the same," said my father, holding up an

intestine for the carpenter to stuff, "those ruins did look uncanny. When I paddled my canoe across the Motława and caught sight of them from a distance, I thought it was like a city on the moon."

Mr. Kaspar shook his head and tied up the stuffed intestine with some fine string. As he was about to say something, about the ruins perhaps, or about that pair of Mennonite eyes, my father looked up and saw me standing in the doorway.

"Isn't he in bed yet?" he cried in amazement. "What time is it?" Mr. Kaspar gestured to him to be silent, put down the washbowl, asked him to keep an eye on the fire—there's nothing worse for cured ham than an uneven stream of smoke —and led me across the garden to the house.

"What about the table?" I asked timidly.

Mr. Kaspar replied that everything would be all right, that there was a right time for everything.

In the distance, from the direction of the river, several voices were hoarsely crooning: "*And then you'll give me a little pity, and then you'll give me a kiss, my pretty!*"

"That's the Ukrainians," explained the carpenter, when we reached the veranda, "from the collective farm on the other side of the river. They drink, they sing, they have a sad time. Do you know why they're sad?"

I didn't know why. We went on standing in front of the house, watching the long shadows of the trees spread across the garden paths.

"It's because of the moon," Mr. Kaspar said. "Whenever it's full, the Ukrainians drink and sing. Even in winter. Once, they walked across the ice to this side and set the shed on fire. That was a long while back, ten years ago. Only the moon seemed bigger then—it always does when there's snow on the ground."

I wanted to tell Mr. Kaspar about our table in a different way from my father, who certainly wouldn't have mentioned the Polaske brothers from Zaspa. But the carpenter hurried away, vanishing like a shadow among the trees.

The wrinkle-faced woman took me to a room in the attic and showed me a bed, but I wasn't sleepy. When I heard her footsteps retreating on the stairs, I went to the window and opened it wide. By now the moon was on the far side of the house and its glow seemed weaker, but the roof of the shed, the trees, and the bright ribbon of the river with the drooping arm of the drawbridge were all clear as day. Only the wreck of the barge was lost from sight, somewhere around the bend among the reeds and rushes. On the opposite shore the Ukrainians had lit a bonfire. I could see their figures weaving in and out of its light and I was sorry I couldn't go there, because their song, drawn out, half incomprehensible, and both sinister and soothing at the same time, was strangely alluring.

I was seized with longing to know everything. Where does the Tuja river flow to? Where was Mr. Kaspar's city? Why weren't the Mennonites willing to take up arms? Did they really all go to heaven? I forgot all about Mr. Polaske, my mother, and the round table, for which we'd come over the pontoon bridge across the Vistula.

As I sat down on the bed, my eyes fell on a wardrobe with carved legs. I opened the door, and among men's jackets, trousers, shirts, and ties, all undoubtedly belonging to Mr. Kaspar, I found a hat that was like no other I'd ever seen before, not even in old photographs. It was black, with a huge brim that folded softly and yieldingly beneath my fingers. I stood in front of the mirror and through the gloom I could see the reflection of my face, which I had never looked at as closely as I did now, a face obscured by the shadow of the black brim, its eyes and lips barely visible, blurred. Meanwhile the hat was getting bigger and bigger, and along with it I was growing. When I was as tall as my father and as broad-shouldered as Mr. Kaspar, I crossed the moonlit garden to the river, went up the wooden gang-plank, and stepped aboard the barge. The draw-bridge raised its arm, and standing at the steering wheel, I guided my ship along the meanders of the Tuja river, the offshoots of canals, through locks and floodgates, until I sailed out onto the Motława. When we docked at Long Harbor in the throng of masts, chimneys, and ensigns, I asked the Ukrainians to unload. Sacks of grain, baskets of apples and plums, barrels with live fish swimming in them, pieces of cloth scented with herbs, and large tubs of butter all made their way from the hold onto the pier. The Ukrainians crooned plaintively as they worked, and though I didn't understand all the words of their song, in which a Mr. Potocki, "*that son of a bitch, betrayed Lithuania, Poland, and all Ukraine,*" I listened to them as if they were a familiar refrain, expressing inconsolable yearning and anger.

The black hat had finally regained its depth and sharpness in the mirror, when I caught sight of a candle flame. Above the broad brim the woman's wrinkled face appeared. She was standing behind me, holding a candlestick, wearing a billowing dressing gown that went down to her ankles. I watched her reflection in the mirror for some time before I saw the tears running down her cheeks. I thought she had been moved by the words of the song that was drifting across from the bonfire on the far side of the river, but that wasn't it. With a delicate movement she took the hat from my head and turned it in her hands.

When had she entered the room and for how long had she been watching me at the mirror? Could she have seen me on the barge?

The candle, set down on the floor, flickered weakly, while the silent woman with a wrinkled face stood beside me and stared at the black hat, thinking thoughts that I couldn't know. Our eyes met on the glassy surface of the mirror, and then she left the room, clutching the hat's black brim with both hands.

I blew out the candle. The starched sheets enfolded me with soothing coolness, and yet I was burning hot, as if I were standing by the oven in the shed where Mr. Kaspar and my father, busy with their illegal butchery, had forgotten all about the passage of time and the world outside.

I didn't exchange a word with the wrinkle-faced woman that night or the next morning, as the two men, breakfasting on smoked bacon and black pudding, discussed the particulars of the order: the diameter of the tabletop, the leg height, and the color of the veneer.

I didn't tell my father about the black hat as we traveled by narrow-gauge railway along the Tuja river, past overgrown canals and closed-down locks, or later, as we streaked across the pontoon bridge over the Vistula in a sky blue bus, not even when the brick church towers loomed ahead in the suburbs of Long Gardens.

As my father was unwrapping some juniper-scented ham from a greasy piece of paper and my mother was nursing a migraine with a damp towel around her head, they shouted words such as "duty," "table," "thoughtlessness," and "opportunity" at each other. I looked at their angry faces and in my thoughts I was with the wrinkled woman: I felt that I would never forget her and she would never forget me.

A week later there was a knock at our door and some strange men carried Mr. Kaspar's table into the living room. It was round, with a walnut veneer, and it utterly enraptured my mother. The squabbling and bickering were forgotten, and that day dinner went on for ages, as if Grandma Maria had come to visit us.

The chestnut trees along our street were in bloom. Bent over Mr. Kaspar's table, I was struggling with the first letters of my reader and getting to know the story of Ala, who has a cat. I was reading the first sentence—"This is a factory"—when Mr. Polaske knocked at our door. Bashfully, he told us how he'd found our address and what troubles he'd had with his visa and with the officials at the Ministry of Foreign Affairs. He sat at Mr. Kaspar's table and took out some coffee, cocoa, chocolate, and a tin of English tea as he told us about his journey and how very happy he was to be here.

"Will you have dinner with us?" asked my mother, but Mr. Polaske was in a hurry to get to his hotel. He said thank you, apologized, and left quickly. My father said good-bye to him at the door.

"He didn't notice the table," said my father.

But I wasn't so sure. This time, the presents he left did not disappear. I turned the pages of the primer. Ala went to school. Dad went to work. Mom cooked dinner. The workers smelted steel. The miners extracted coal. The pilot flew over the motherland. The Vistula flowed to the Baltic. The woman took away the black hat. The Mennonites went straight to heaven. Mr. Polaske sold a table, and Mr. Kaspar made a new one.

"What are you reading? He's making it up, isn't he?" asked my mother.

"Yes, yes." My father lit a cigarette, and put his hand on the table as the light slid along its surface. "It's all made up. Every word of it."

I gazed at the trail of smoke dwindling toward the ceiling. From then on time passed differently, and only I knew why.

Snails, Puddles, Rain

■ ■ ■

To Franco Rossetti

In the beginning was the rain. It had been falling
for several days, and near the church of the Resurrection Fathers the water had gouged out deep
channels down which twigs, blades of grass, and
little pinecones from the forest went sailing. I
liked to stand there. The water gurgled over
stones washed from the path, and the rivulets all
ran together into a single rapid torrent which
flowed down Gomółka Street, then cut across
Chrzanowski Road, and flooded out into enormous puddles on both sides of the road. The hills
beyond the church were shrouded in mist, heavy
drops fell continuously from the branches of pine
trees and spruces, and everything, even the roofs
of the houses and the top of the church's wooden
belfry, was drowned in the monotonous roar of
the stream.

Every year the scent of summer blew inland
from the sea. The breeze carried the smell of nets
hung out to dry, and the taste of salt which you

could feel on your lips. But now the summer was showing its other face, perhaps a secret face. Something invisible hung over the earth, and in it a force of fertility. The fragrance of mildew, mushrooms, resin, and unfamiliar herbs wafted over the puddles like a dense concoction, it came back with every new wave of rain; it filled the streets and gardens, and burgeoning greenery seemed about to tear apart the soaked tenement walls from which the plaster had been peeling for years, revealing occasional snippets of indecipherable inscriptions.

From my pocket I pulled the pieces of wood I'd prepared. First on the water was the *Santa Maria*, then the *Magellan*, the *Captain Grant*, and the *Nautilus*, and in between came the *Tempest*, the World War II destroyer. As the finale to my launching, I set afloat my flagship, the *Trinidad*. The name didn't come from a book or from a sailor's stories—*Trinidad* expressed nostalgia for the warmth of tropical seas, the glitter of Spanish gold, and the scent of mandarins, which sometimes turned up in our town before Christmas, when a ship from Greece or Portugal put in to the harbor.

Here and there a splotch of black cassock showed through the jungle of greenery. It was the priest, coming down to the church from his house on the hill, carrying an enormous umbrella. He brushed off the raindrops, flapping his arms like a great bird beating its black wings, then stopped on the steps. He looked up at the sky and down at the road, but our gazes didn't cross.

Faster and faster sailed the ships, as the water carried them over whirlpools, waterfalls, and foaming cataracts; I ran after them all the way down to the point where the stream flowed far and wide, not hissing or gurgling any more, and my armada came sailing out onto broad, calm waters. The puddles had a dark green tinge that turned to bronze when the sky grew cloudier than usual; then the vivid hulls of the *Santa Maria* and the *Nautilus* stood out like horizontal dashes.

I waded among the puddles like God stooping over the Earth. Islands, bays, promontories, headlands, and secret isthmuses were constantly changing shape. Time and again the line of a Norwegian fjord or the shape of the Swedish coast would appear, only to undergo mysterious change in a matter of moments. Whole countries disintegrated in the blink of an eye, skerries and shallows defined new navigation lanes, and new archipelagos took the place of old ones, their contours so fantastically intricate that no map could ever render such finesse and subtle beauty. Among them I discovered my ships again. Some

were rolling on the water, others had run
aground in the shallows, and only the Trinidad, as
if its name were a summons to the ultimate voyage, was speeding through the flood waters, an
invisible current sweeping it away to the far ends
of the earth. This was a dangerous place. The water roared against the concrete threshold, and everything, even small stones and clods of yellow
clay, was sucked in by the mighty whirlpool of
the drain whose cast-iron lid led down to an underworld where the light of day did not pene-
trate—a labyrinth of caverns and slimy walls
filled with hissing and roaring. Water squished in
my galoshes as, at the very last moment, I fished
out the Trinidad, saving hapless voyagers from ca-
tastrophe. Once it was a golden beetle clinging to
the hull, at other times it was a spider or an ant;
I'd transfer the shipwreck victims onto dry land
and wander back uphill, all the way to the
church, where with open umbrella the priest
walked to and fro among the trees, reciting his
breviary.

I was alone and happy. My father was alone as
well, but those days he certainly wasn't happy.
He put on a brave face. He would hum a tune
while shaving, and walk with a spring in his step,
smiling as he nodded to the neighbors. But every
time he went out in the morning, with his breakfast and his orange jacket in his linen bag, off to

work at the train station, where he swept the platforms and the steps with a long broom, I could
see a shade of melancholy in his eyes, a mixture
of sadness and disbelief at the fact that for several
weeks now he was no longer sitting at a vast
drawing board covered in diagrams of ships,
drawing complex lines on tracing paper, and jotting down his comments, figures, square brack-
ets, and square roots—all he'd been doing was
pushing that black broom back and forth, sweeping butts and cores onto a metal shovel while the
wind puffed out his orange jacket as if it were
the flag of a shipwrecked man.

"But you could have signed it," my mother
said every morning. My father would flap about,
shaving cream splattering into the milk pan, but
none of his words—about how figures and calculations can't conform to several languages because there's only one language of mathematics,
as plain and straightforward as Cartesian thought,
and about people who know the terminology of
launching but nothing of the laws of physics—
got through to her; they flowed over her like water and bounced off her like little round balls,
making him even more lonely and desolate.

"That crankshaft will crack after twenty
knots," he went on, doing his best to explain,
but it was hopeless. My mother was not concerned with crankshafts but with the singular os-

tentation with which my father swept the station. Why was he doing it? Why was he tempting fate? It was an open challenge to the people who'd thrown him out, she said as she fueled up the stove with pine chips, and they'd never forgive him for that, they never forgot that sort of thing. Then my father would say how nice it was at the station, whenever the stationmaster waved his red lollypop, whenever they announced trains coming from inland, whenever he had a chat with the workmen from the loading platform, who knew exactly what goods would soon appear in the shops, because everything—refrigerators, meat grinders, Czech vacuum cleaners, Yugoslav furniture, Persian carpets from East Germany, you name it—passed through their hands, and they could go on about it for hours, inspired, as they sat waiting for the next shipment to come in.

"I've never seen a Czech vacuum cleaner," cried my mother, "and I've certainly never seen an engineer boast about a job like that one." Before my father could make it out of the house she'd add that coming to this city had been all a mistake, that spending their afternoons carrying rubble from the ruins all had been a mistake, and rebuilding them like thousands of others with song and cheer, since now my father couldn't find suitable work here—wherever he showed his face they'd throw up their hands and say, "Do forgive us, please, but with your views . . ." as if crankshafts had anything to do with views.

Making his exit, my father would say that working at the station was wonderful and that there was really nothing to get so upset about; as soon as they finished building that ship and took it for a test run, they'd see who was right. The truth would come to light, because the truth always floats to the surface, like oil.

"What truth?" my mother would ask, but he'd be out of earshot, he'd be off across the yard, his head bowed as he leaped across the puddles, his linen bag swinging from his shoulder. Yet I could feel that each day he was more lonely than the day before, and that he was just putting a brave face on it. After all, a station platform is hardly the same as the blueprint of a hull or an engine-room, and a broom could never substitute for the black graphite pencil he used to jot down all those figures and calculations.

We were both alone, each in his own way— he in his orange jacket like the ones the trash collectors wore, tracing the shapes of pistons, valve outlets, crankshafts, and fuel inlets with his broom, and I, watching the stream of rain water on its journey to the far ends of the earth, all the way down to the point where the dark hole sucked in all objects along with the surging torrent.

Could this be what the way to Hades looked like? I knew that the world of shades, hidden from the eyes of mortals, had secret entrances, back gates known only to the courageous few, but did the path to the kingdom of Persephone come this way? If I were Odysseus or the Thracian bard, could I tip up the lid of the drain and in a single step find myself on the banks of the river Styx? The only person who would know was Grandma Maria, who used to read me mythology on her winter visits; she alone would have agreed to be led across the massive puddles and would surely have admired the whirlpool into which all the living creatures carried along by the water disappeared. But she wasn't with me, she wasn't even in our city; she lived far away. As I waded about the flood waters, I had nothing to fall back on but guesses, uncertainties, and the silent glances of the priest.

If the Lord Jesus had spent three days after his burial in Hades, if he had tamed Cerberus with a single gesture and met ill-starred Sisyphus, then I could have asked the priest about the secret way into the Underworld. But as I stood over the drain, a laconic, mysterious sentence from the Credo uttered at every Mass came to me: "And He descended into Hell, and on the third day He rose again." It said nothing more precise than that about Hell, nor did it give any indication of whether Hell had anything in common with Hades and the waters of forgetfulness. In spite of that, I could imagine Jesus in the flowing waters. Dressed in white robes, his hand raised aloft and his side bared to show the marks of the nails and the Roman spear, he was sailing across in Charon's boat, amid mists and swirling phantoms. I found this vision especially beautiful and entrancing.

I felt even greater rapture imagining the scene with Sisyphus. Without a word Jesus went and helped him roll the boulder up the hill, and when at last Sisyphus cried out in amazement, "I did it! I did it!" Jesus emerged from a mist-cloud and said in a booming voice, for everyone to hear: "Sisyphus! Your sins are forgiven!" Then Jesus continued on, all the way to the Garden of the Hesperides, where among the swaying branches, the golden apples, and the gentle breeze, the poets strolled, among them my Grandfather Karol, who never actually wrote any poems but who had the soul of a poet and was sure to be wandering in the tall grass with the other shades.

The water flowed on incessantly, reflecting clouds heavy with rain, while I waded in the green puddles that spiraled around the drain well for hours on end, watching the way the surface of the water reflected not just trees and sky but also my thoughts, thoughts I could never have revealed to the Reverend Father but which I kept safe and secret for Grandma Maria. The priest's voice was stern during Sunday school when he spoke about false prophets, imaginary gods, and nonexistent kingdoms, while Grandma Maria's voice was soft and warm when she told stories of Odysseus or the voyage of the Argonauts as if they'd happened not so long ago, as if their nimble ships had often sailed across our bay, their oars cleaving the water, their purple sails billowing. The waters of forgetfulness might well have sprung from this very spot, near the church of the Resurrection Fathers. Leaning over the stream, I set my ships afloat closer and closer to the point of danger, until at last the gurgling whirlpool had engulfed the *Nautilus* and the *Tempest*, sucked in the *Santa Maria* and the *Magellan*, and swallowed the *Captain Grant*; only the *Trinidad*, my flagship, which was once to set sail for the Antilles in search of Spanish gold and the scent of mandarins, only the Trinidad, with its exotic-sounding name like a word on a foreign postage stamp, emerged from these trials triumphant.

I went home inspired. The scent of moist earth, of mud and slime rose over the waters and hovered like an invisible bird, higher and higher, finally enfolding the port, the bay, the shipyards, and the church towers in the spread of its phantom wings. I paused next to some houses where the words *Butter-Milch-Brot* and *Tabakenhandlung* were still visible under layers of plaster. I gazed at rusted awnings, twisting cast-iron railings topped with spikes shaped like candle flames; I stopped by gardens gone to seed, where in the under-growth of weeds and massive burdock leaves lurked the wooden figures of gnomes, swans, and long-haired princesses; I stared at green, moss-covered summerhouses, overgrown with wisteria or wild vine; I skipped lightly across the puddles, dodged the fire hydrants, and thought about Grandfather Karol, who didn't like coming to our city. I thought about my father, who loved this city, and I thought about myself, standing be-tween them, like someone at a crossroads peering at a signpost whose letters have long since been erased by the water, sand, and wind.

"My God, what on earth have you been doing?" said my mother. "Where have you been all day?" But these were rhetorical questions.

I'd dry my feet by the kitchen stove and have a look through the Sea Annuals, full of drawings of sailing ships. My father would come back from the station tired and taciturn. We'd have some potato soup; the second course would be potatoes and cauliflower. Sometimes we ate dessert as well. Then my father would go into the living room and switch on the Beethoven or the Pioneer radio show: he'd fall asleep to the sound of music or the afternoon news. I knew that when he woke up, my mother would start questioning him about that wretched crankshaft again, going on about his signature or rather the lack of his signature on the blueprints. Then he'd start pacing up and down the room waving his arms about like a preacher; he'd raise his voice, then lower it down to a whisper. He'd explained it all before, hadn't he?—the managing directors' haste, the launching deadline, all that fuss about the *Marshal Zhukov* wasn't worth a thing because you can't build a ship faster than is physically possible, and the same goes for blueprints riddled with mistakes that no one wants to talk about, although they had plenty to say about a well-known friendship for a certain nation and about suspect elements who refused to recognize that friendship and were retarding the swift march of progress into the marvelous twenty-first century.

"Well, they can do it without me," my father would say. To regain his good mood, he'd bring out a box of photographs. Grandfather Karol would appear at the table, in the uniform of a *Leutenant* of the Austro-Hungarian Imperial artillery, and beside him Baron von Moll with puttees and a saber stuck into the ground. Both held tankards of frothing beer; behind them you could see the barrel of an enormous cannon, and like a couple of gentlemen taking the waters at a spa they were smiling to the strains of the *Radetzky March*. So it went until the very last photograph, in which Grandfather Karol was standing by himself against a backdrop of burned-out houses, wearing the insignia of an *Oberleutenant* and no longer looking at us as cheerfully as before because all that was left of Baron von Moll was a shapeless lump of meat—though then again it may have been because he was no longer holding a tankard of beer and behind him the city was in flames.

"That's Gorlice," said my father, "in 1915, the year of the Austrian offensive in the Eastern Carpathians. And that's your grandfather with President Mościcki," he'd say, passing me the next picture, "in free Poland by then, when they opened the factory near Tarnów."

I looked at Grandfather Karol, standing beside the President in his tailcoat and top hat; although he wasn't holding a tankard of beer, his eyes were smiling, just as in the picture of him and Grandma Maria coming out of Lwów cathedral, he in his tailcoat, minus the topper, and she in a white dress and a white hat, carrying a bouquet of lily-of-the-valley. Her face, free of wrinkles in the full sunlight of a Lwów afternoon, was not the same one I knew from winter evenings in our

apartment when she read me stories from Par-
andowski's book about the wanderings of Odysseus or the beautiful Helen. But the scent of
lily-of-the-valley went everywhere with her, in-
variably, as if she'd carried that bouquet her
whole life long, hidden away in her handbag.

My father would lose himself in meditation
over these photographs. Their tawny tones had a
melancholy effect on him. He never looked at all
of them in one sitting; he'd sigh and put them
away in their box.

"Next time," he'd say softly, and go into the
kitchen where he'd smoke a cigarette and spend
all evening drinking tea.

My mother would make the bed, rain drum-
ming against the windowpanes, while I thought
about the faces in the photographs, especially
those of the strangers whose names weren't given
in the beautiful copperplate writing on the back
of the yellowed card. The man in a white apron
serving beer to Grandfather Karol and Baron von
Moll smiled at me knowingly, as if he knew what
they were chatting about in front of that inn in
Upper Moravia, whereas the woman in a black
toque and veil standing behind President Mościcki looked at me questioningly, as if I were supposed to divine her fate before or after that
moment. The man on the steps of the Lwów cathedral was vague and distant; he'd certainly got

there by accident and was observing Grandma Maria and Grandfather Karol's wedding by chance, though he could also have been a belated guest, one of those people who are always late for everything, even for their own funerals.

As I fell asleep, I could still see those strange faces, which gradually disappeared into the darkness, like my ships into the abyss of the drain. Even in my dreams I wandered around that spot; I waded in the dark green water and put my ear to the invisible cascade, listening intently to its ceaseless roar, its splashing and gurgling, and I felt more and more inhibited by the gaze of the priest, watchful and vigilant, as if over there, on the other side, some force lay hidden which shouldn't be disturbed.

Neither my father nor I, stooping over the slots in the cast-iron lid which I didn't have the courage to lift, had the slightest inkling that the snail season was approaching, and at a rapid pace.

One day I saw my father all the way up the street. He was walking slowly, his head drooping; his bag hung from his shoulder like an empty sack, and when I ran up to ask him what he'd talked about today with the workmen on the loading platform and why he was home from the station so early, he said, "I'm not going to sweep the platforms any more."

This was no bitter or heroic declaration; the

tone of his voice was flat, or maybe sad. As we
went past the chestnut trees, which radiated a
pleasant coolness and respite in the heat—that
day their leaves were rustling with raindrops—
my father told me how that morning two men
had turned up at the station and informed the
stationmaster who my father was. They had stated
categorically that as an engineer he couldn't work
there—it was an open provocation "leveled at
progress and achievement." Afterwards the stationmaster asked my father into his office, laughing. "You really took me in!" he said, bouncing
up and down in his chair. "You're a real joker!"
he chuckled. "Well, I'm very sorry, but you can't
go on working here, I'm sure you understand . . ."
As we were going through the front door of our
building, my father explained to me that on the
Polish State Railways employment questionnaire
he had written "unqualified workman," which,
although it wasn't the truth, was justified because, after all, he couldn't find work as an
engineer any more.

"Well, then," said my mother, adopting a busi-
nesslike tone, "we're emigrating to America!
They build ships there, too, better than the *Marshal
Zhukov*!"

As my mother mulled over passports, visas,
and money, as she wondered how, without the

necessary influence and push to obtain the unob-
tainable, not to mention tickets for the transatlantic liner that was to carry us to the foot of the
Statue of Liberty, my father seemed even more
desolate and lonely.

Like him, I wasn't enthusiastic about sailing to
America; I didn't want to swap my street lined
with chestnut trees for the Statue of Liberty or
some skyscrapers. I had no desire to chew gum,
play baseball, or watch Mickey Mouse films,
which I didn't like at all. So I felt all the more
drawn to him. We would spend long hours bent
over sheets of paper on which, with a steady
hand, he drew me the cruiser *Spalato*, the ironclad
Kaiser Max, or the frigate *Radetzky*—it was those
ships most often, because Grandma Maria's father
Tadeusz had served on them, as a mechanic in
the Austro-Hungarian Imperial Navy.

"The *Spalato*," said my father, "fifty-five meters
in length, eight meters wide, with a displacement
of three and seven-tenths, and torpedo launchers
and armament from Krupp's added to that, just
look what they're like!" And out of the box he
took a photograph of my great-grandfather Tadeusz standing on the deck of the *Spalato* in the
uniform of an engineer cadet, probably somewhere in Trieste or Pula, one arm around Mr.
Ferdynand Karolka, another cadet, and the other

around a mechanic called Julius von Petravic, which sounded odd because the "von" didn't go with the Croatian "Petravic."

"This ship," said my father, falling into a reverie, "once sailed to India with Rear Admiral Manfronim, in 1889 or maybe 1890—we'll have to check that." He drew the next photograph from the box. In this one, Great-Grandfather was wearing not the uniform of the Imperial Navy but an elaborate overcoat, and he was looking at us with a deep, intent expression. In the bottom margin there was an inscription in silver: *Atelier Artistique Photographique—Stella.* I was fascinated by the shape of the letters and by the double-headed eagle of the Monarchy, also in silver. "Lwów, 3rd of May, 1911," I read out slowly.

Next he showed me a postcard with a view of the Polytechnic Institute, where the former cadet had lectured on physics and mechanics and became a professor and, in time, a court privy counsellor. And I began to imagine him striding along Hetman's Embankment in that overcoat of his, passing the Sobieski monument, acacia flowers gently falling on his graying, close-cropped hair and the lapels of his overcoat. I could see him clearly in that strange, unfamiliar city, which was called Lwów, or Lemberg, or Lviv, a city which had a Polytechnic Institute, a theater, and a railway station, but no port or shipyards. Suddenly

I understood why, as soon as the war had ended, my father came to Gdańsk and enrolled in the Polytechnic Institute to study the construction of ship engines.

My mother went on sending letters to Warsaw, to offices, government departments, and consulates, but somehow there was no answer. Meanwhile, every morning my father scanned the paper, reading the obituary notices, the weather forecast, and the classified columns. There, in the classified ads section, among the things for sale —a secondhand washing machine, a winter coat with astrakhan collar and cuffs, some begonia seedlings—he came across the Roman snails which had been waiting for us since the beginning of summer.

"High prices," he said one day, smiling enigmatically, then put on his coat and left the house. When he came back two hours later, his smile lit up the entire flat, as if it had suddenly stopped raining and the wind had driven away all the clouds above our city and the bay. "Tomorrow we'll get down to work," he announced. "And if you'll help me, we can earn a bit of money."

"It's disgusting," my mother cut him short. She wasn't thinking of the money, but of the snails, hidden among leaves and grass, which we were going to gather. "How can you possibly put that in your mouth?"

"Maybe you can't," my father agreed, "unless you're French." Then he enthusiastically explained that after we were paid for them, the Roman snails would go straight to Paris, and there, properly prepared, would be served as a rare delicacy, a sophisticated hors d'oeuvre, because the French are a fastidious nation, they don't put just anything in their mouths as—with all respect—we do, or as the Russians do, especially.

The next day, in galoshes and raincoats, we set off for the forest, baskets in hand, passing the church of the Resurrection Fathers on the way. When the priest waved to us and called out, "Good mushrooming!" my father replied, "May God requite you!" Soon after that he was bending over a clump of fern to pull the first Roman snail from the soggy grass. He turned it delicately in his fingers, examining the shape of its shell and horns, then put it in the basket filled with leaves and moved on, as if he'd done nothing else his whole life. As I walked after him, I felt myself entering another world. With no regrets I abandoned the stream and the puddles, the spot where the secret gate into the Underworld lay hidden underwater, and my ships and the Austro-Hungarian Imperial Navy on the Adriatic. From the moment my father put the first snail in his basket—he found it beneath a clump of fern just beyond the church of the Resurrection Fathers—

I hadn't the slightest doubt that there was nothing ordinary about this way of earning money.

From then on, every evening my father would spread out a huge map with the caption *Freistadt Danzig* on the table; then he'd draw a circle on it with his finger, saying, "We haven't been here yet," as I haltingly spelled out, "Stolzenberg, Luftkurort Oliva, Nawitzweg, Glettkau, Langfuhr." To my amazement I found that these strange names simply stood for Pohulanka, Oliwa, Dolne Mlyny near Brętowo, Jelitkowo, or Wrzeszcz; then I noticed, to my even greater amazement, that some of them had withstood the war, migrations, and fires with only slight alterations in sound: Ohra had changed into Orunia, Brosen had become Brzeźno, Schidlitz was now Siedlce. What amazed me most of all in this snail's geography were the places whose names hadn't changed at all, places that had stuck with their original names like old people keeping to well-trodden paths. As we wandered the hills of Emaus, criss-crossed by crevices, with a view of the bay and the ships, or as we fished snails out of the undergrowth in the abbey park at Oliwa, I thought about the story which features the looking-glass Sea of Galilee instead of the bay, and a garden of olive trees instead of the abbey park.

"Do you think He could have come this way?" I asked my father. Deep in thought, he turned his gaze away from the leaves, grass, and snails, and in a quiet voice said that anything is possible; our senses can mislead us and quite often mock our judgement, so you can't rely on them too much—you might as easily see something that doesn't exist as fail to see something that does.

"Besides," he concluded, raising his index finger, "there are things we've never even dreamed of, far beyond the limits of our imagination, yet which undoubtedly exist around us without our knowing it."

I wasn't entirely satisfied with this answer. If my father had just said Yes or No, it would have been much simpler. I couldn't understand why our eyes would mislead us, or our hearing or sense of touch either. As we were coming down from the hills of Emaus along a sandy path lined with tall lime trees, I asked if the things we see and hear and touch really do exist: the red roofs of the houses, these ancient trees, the sound of the rain or the violet mantle of the bay spread out far beneath our feet beyond the line of cranes and shipyard gantries.

My father bent down to the path and picked up a Roman snail. Contemplating its shell, he said, "It can't be proved. It's not a mathematical equation. But you realize"—the snail went into the basket and I felt my father's hand on my shoulder—"there is someone who sees to it that we don't go astray. Someone who shows us the way."

"God?" I asked.

"Yes," he answered softly, and his yes was so simple, clear, and plain that I had no more questions to ask, as if over the hills of Emaus and over our entire city an invisible gaze had suddenly unfurled, which wouldn't let us go astray and would ensure that everything around us was wonderfully real—the snails, the leaves, the puddles, and the drops of water streaming down my father's raincoat.

In the afternoons we'd stop at a green hut where, hobbling along on his wooden leg, Mr. Kosterke would weigh the snails, make notes with a graphite pencil on greasy bits of paper, ask my father to sign, and give us some money. Five-zloty pieces with a fisherman dragging his nets, coins with the likeness of Tadeusz Kościuszko, and sometimes even a red banknote bearing the face of a worker all made their way into my father's pocket. Meanwhile I'd take a good look at Mr. Kosterke, whose nose was as upturned as Tadeusz Kościuszko's and who spoke in a thick German accent and smelled of drink and tobacco. Once the snails had been put in a special box lined with grass and leaves, my father would sit down on a

rickety bench and invite Mr. Kosterke to have a
cigarette. They would start chatting about the
weather and the snail market, then they'd pick up
speed and leap across national and economic borders, founding the greatest Roman snail-buying
firm in Central Europe, amassing enormous sums
of money, opening up more and more new mar-
kets, and finally building a snail cannery with the
poetic name of "Laura," because that was the
name of Mr. Kosterke's wife, with whom he had
run a store on the corner of Hubertusbürgerallee
before the war.

"Where was that?" asked my father. "I don't
think I've ever seen it on my map." Mr. Kosterke
spoke of a crossroads on the way out of town and
a shop where he sold groceries from all over the
world. He talked about his wife and daughters,
and about how he was all alone now with his
wooden leg. He had lost the real one in 1946
when he'd stepped on a German mine, which
was the real reason he hadn't left for Germany—
he didn't make it on time for the last train, and
after that he lost the desire to leave, afraid he
might accidentally lose the other, good leg. It was
very difficult when people said that he, Kosterke,
was a German—after all, he was a citizen of
Gdańsk and spoke Polish almost as well as he did
German.

"Hubertusbürgerallee," said my father, mus-

ing. "That's a fine name. Yes, I'll have to look for
that street." Then Mr. Kosterke would come limp-
ing out of the depths of the hut with a bottle and
a couple of glasses, and they'd drink each other's
health as if they'd been close friends for years.
I'd watch their faces twisting harshly as they
snacked on pickled cucumber fished out of a jar
with dill, a cherry leaf, and a clove of garlic floating in it. I knew we'd never leave for America in
search of money and freedom, because we did
have something to eat after all, thanks to the
snails. Criss-crossing the hills of Emaus, ferreting
about in the Strzyża valley or tramping the hill-
ocks in the Oliwa forest, my father and I knew
real freedom.

"The snail season will be coming to an end
soon," Mr. Kosterke said one day. "I'll be going
back to my bottles and waste paper. What about
you?"

My father shrugged his shoulders.

"I might start building a boat," he said, turning the empty glass in his hand, "and we'll sail
off on a long voyage. That would be much better for my son than school. The Kiel Canal, the
English Channel, then the Bay of Biscay and
Gibraltar," he reeled off in a single breath. "The
Mediterranean, the Aegean, and finally Ithaca!
We'll sail around Ithaca and then come home
again, and we'll send you postcards, Mr. Koster-

ke, from Hamburg and Marseilles. What do you think of that?"

The former merchant from Hubertusbürgerallee looked at us in silence. Suddenly, as if at the touch of an invisible hand, the threads of time began to interweave in the air of the wooden hut, and the dark interior of the shop was filled with the smell of coffee, cinnamon, ginger and nutmeg, cloves and Moselle wine. Mr. Kosterke had his real leg again and was standing behind a gleaming oak counter smoking a Vineta cigarette from the Danziger Tabak Monopol Aktiongesellschaft, and on the other side of the counter my father was smoking a small Okassa Zarotto cigar, bought at Kummer's store next to the Green Gate, a cigar from Halpaus's factory in Wrocław. My father asked Mr. Kosterke, "How's business?" and the grocer replied that it wasn't what it used to be; ever since the Brown Shirts had taken over the streets of our free city and had begun waging a tariff war with Poland, business hadn't been going too well. The gulden was falling headlong, and he was thinking of opening an account for himself in some Polish bank in Gdynia, which wasn't entirely legal but was lucrative, since the Polish zloty stood strong, without the slightest wobble, like the Swiss franc. In his fingers my father turned the Okassa Zarotto box, adorned with the portrait of a beautiful woman who gazed up at him; her naked shoulders, her classical profile, the arches of her brows, and the locks of her black hair crowned with an orchid exuded the mysterious, alluring air of the Levant. Mr. Kosterke, his voice lowered, told the story of National Socialist Party dignitaries like Rauschnig, President of the Free Town Senate, who had withdrawn their money from the Gdańsk banks and invested it in Polish ones on the other side of the border, and of how the Social Democrats had been beaten up by the Brown Shirts at a rally and the Christian Democrats had been put in jail. He said, in a complete whisper now, that hard times were approaching for Jews and Poles and all decent people, while my father drank in the woman's Grecian profile, her slender neck and smooth cheeks, as if the medallion with her portrait was not just a label on the Okassa Zarotto box, but a miniature painted by Mehoffer, the same one that hung over Great-Grandfather Tadeusz's desk in the apartment on Ujejski Street in Lwów, depicting his Hungarian wife from the Shegivi family, who died in her youth.

"Yes, yes," my father responded, "there are hard times ahead of us, but has it ever really been any easier?"

The scent of ginger, nutmeg, cloves, and Turkish tobacco evaporated imperceptibly, and so did the blue and yellow packet of Vineta cigarettes and the Okassa Zarotto box. Mr. Kosterke, with his wooden leg again, leaned toward my father and whispered some secret information in his ear:

"You'll find the greatest amount of them in the cemeteries, especially overgrown, closed-down ones—they're creatures of the cemetery, I tell you! And I'll tell you why. The bushes and leaves there have a special flavor because they absorb slightly better juices from the earth. The snails can sense that, so before the season ends that's where you'll gather the most."

Raindrops began to fall on the roof of the hut. Mr. Kosterke put the bottle away behind the counter while my father listened to the advice about Roman snails and cemeteries in disbelief, until at last he said politely that we had to go now because it was getting late.

"What nonsense!" he said on the way home. "Snails live wherever there's vegetation, that's all!"

The next few days threw us into a state of utter confusion. On the way back from Lower Mills via Brętowo we stopped at the edge of an old cemetery where, among overgrown tombstones with inscriptions in German and shattered angels and moldering crosses entwined in knotgrass, we stumbled upon a veritable kingdom of snails. We had to be careful not to step on the shells that lay hidden in the tall grass, and we only had to draw back a branch of wild elder or honeysuckle to reveal whole clans of Roman snails, all glued to one another, three or four at a time, as if they feared loneliness or were performing some sort of love rite.

Not just our baskets but also our spare gray canvas bag were soon brimming full of them. My father said nothing, but when Mr. Kosterke paid us several red banknotes with a worker's face on them, I said that perhaps the Roman snails were envoys from the Underworld.

"Nonsense!" said my father, with a note of irritation. "How did you ever get that idea into your head?"

But when, the following day, we passed near the Polytechnic Institute and, as if unintentionally, entered the overgrown alleyways of a cemetery where Germans were once buried but where nowadays no one but drunks and tramps went, we found among the weeping willows, hornbeams, copper beeches, and spruces even more Roman snails than in Brętowo. My father couldn't contain himself.

"There really is something odd about this," he said, "but does it have any connection with death?"

I didn't know how to answer. The world of snails was silent and inaccessible. Their trails, marked by a silvery thread, seemed especially mysterious. Could the fact that they lived in this particular place really have some connection with, for example, Hugo Toller, who died in Wrzeszcz in 1938, on the seventeenth of October? Or with a certain Doctor Merz, musician and conductor, who went to his eternal rest at the very end of the war, but before the houses, granaries, and churches of the Old Town had burned down and turned to dust? I asked my father what "gone to his eternal rest" meant. Is it a union with God? And where is the place we call eternity? Is it up there, above us? Or down below? Is eternity all around us, except that we can't see it, just as we can't see the air which is all around us and which we breathe without even thinking about it?

My father was putting snails into the baskets.

"All I know is that God exists and that we all fear death," he said after a moment's reflection. "The rest is pure guesswork."

"Are you afraid of death, too?" I asked.

"I am," he answered.

"So what's it like, when you die?"

He didn't reply at once. I could see that he wanted to explain something properly. He was thinking hard, as if laboring over an equation with several unknowns.

"Motion is a mystery, you see? The movement of particles, bodies. Where there's no motion,

there's no life either. Death is the cessation of
motion in every way and form. You understand?"

I nodded, and as he wandered about in the
knee-high grass, he went on to say that death
means a state in which all pain and suffering have
ceased, so from one point of view, for some people, it might be a desirable thing. A state of absolute peace and quiet, which we can't even
begin to imagine.

But I could imagine that quietness. I could see
it, like a great sheet spread out over our city, over
the hills and the bay, with everyone sleeping beneath it—Grandfather Karol, Great-Grandfather
Tadeusz and his young wife, Karolka, the cadet,
Baron von Moll and the mechanic, von Petravic,
the woman in the black toque and veil who stood
behind President Mościcki, and the man from the
Lwów cathedral steps—all the people I'd never
known and couldn't ever know were immersed
in a massive silence, which the snails crept across
in their mottled shells, sticking their horns out
ahead of them to catch the voices of the dead.

From day to day my father grew more reticent,
perhaps because the snail season was coming to
an end, or maybe because of the neighbors, who
had found out about our occupation and had
taken to swapping none-too-clever comments on

it. But on the last day, which was St. John's day, my father did start to show signs of satisfaction.

"Let's get the snails over with," he said. "The French can worry about them now."

As we wandered around Bishop's Hill, scouring the bushes and wild alleyways of the park on our last search for snails, my father said that we'd earned quite a lot of money and wouldn't have to worry about the coming month.

"I could do this all year round," I said. "I could walk around with you like this forever, and if we ran out of snails, we could gather herbs and dry them to sell to sick people."

"Yes," he said, smiling, "that's a good idea. If we ever run short of money again, we'll do that."

To earn our final snail fee and be sure to take home several red banknotes that evening to put on the table in front of my mother, we bustled among the bushes like a proper pair of hunters, plunging into dense tunnels of greenery that had been wet and damp since the start of summer, so busy that we didn't notice twilight coming on, and with it shop-closing time.

"Never mind," said my father. "In that case, we'll set them free."

Before he put the basket down, we saw a most unusual thing. Dozens of snails were crawling out from under the bushes, abandoning their hide-outs and making off in the same direction, to-ward the top of the hill. More of them kept appearing, not dozens, but hundreds.

"Look over here," cried my father. "And here, over here, too." He grew even more excited. "They're on parade!"

Sure enough, one behind another, horns held aloft, the snails were creeping toward the hilltop as if they had an appointment up there.

"I've never seen anything like it. Come on," my father said. "We've got to see where they're heading."

The creeping line of snails was a weird sight. The closer they got to the hill, the more snails joined the procession, and when the path reached the clearing, it was entirely covered in moving shells.

"Like eels in the Sargasso Sea," I heard my fa-ther whisper. "There's some sort of mystery be-hind it."

But what we saw at the summit was even more surprising. In the middle of the clearing a gigantic stone rose straight out of the ground, one of the many that were scattered about the hills by a gla-cier. Its steep sides rose to the height of a man, and it was shaped like a huge tear that only a mythical giant could have shed. Cautiously, almost on tiptoe to avoid stepping on the snails, we approached the rock. Then we stopped as if we ourselves had turned to stone.

"My God, what are they doing?" my father said quietly.

One after another the snails were attempting to crawl up the stone's steep gray sides to its summit. The attempt was in vain, however; they couldn't contend with the smooth surface of an almost sheer wall or with the force of gravity, which kept dragging them back down, so they were cascading onto the grass in a swirl of tangled shells and bodies that grated and rustled like a rising and falling wave. Not one of the snails could clamber higher than halfway up the stone, and the silver threads of slime that traced their climb coated the surface of the basalt like transparent armor.

Hypnotized by this swirl of snails, we didn't notice that the rain had stopped and that fireflies were flitting out of the blackness of bushes and undergrowth, blinking all around the clearing. When we finally turned away from the stone, our eyes were met by the sight of tiny whirling flames, spinning faster and faster in the darkness to the rhythm of strange music.

"They'll never get up the stone," said my father, pointing at the snails. "And we'll never know why they have to get there. If one of them were to manage it, something would have to change."

"What?" I asked quietly.

"I don't know. But something would happen."

"To what?" I asked even more quietly.

"To the world, perhaps. I don't know," said my father, emptying the baskets. "But we'd better get out of here. There's no need to disturb them."

As we went down the hill with our empty baskets, and later, when the moon had risen over the city and we were traveling on the night tram past the Sobieski monument and the Polytechnic Institute, I noticed the same shadow of melancholy that appeared in his eyes when he looked at the old photographs or drew sketches of imperial battleships on bits of paper. I realized that we'd never gather snails again and that we would never allude to the clearing and the tall stone in our conversations, because the seal of secrecy had been set on what we saw.

However, that didn't mean the next few days would consist of nothing but puddles and rain. My father mooned about the house, combing the classified ads again, my mother went on writing letters that never got any answers, and as soon as I found a Roman snail in the garden, I made a special pen for it, walled with four bricks beneath the currant bush, and tried to fathom its snaily secrets. Every morning I greeted it with a fresh leaf, and every day I spent hours in the garden watching its behavior and movements. Ignorant of its language, the system of signals floating on invisible airwaves which it picked up with its horns, I tried speaking to it in my own tongue, in the hope that eventually it would understand at least a word or two. Indeed, after some time the snail reacted to my voice and no longer stayed hidden in its shell when I put it on my hand, but that was all I managed to achieve. It did not heed my efforts, and the world of the snail remained unfathomable to me.

The first days of school didn't affect our communication much. I still brought him lettuce leaves and tried to engage him in conversation. Finally one night there was a torrential downpour, and as dawn was breaking, a sharp ground frost set in. I ran down the stairs like a madman and rushed across the rime-cloaked garden, but it was too late. Under the currant bush the white mirror of a frozen puddle had closed over the snail like a glass coffin lid. I scraped the frost off the limpid pane. There at the bottom, like a ball of crystal, lay my prisoner, motionless and dead. A ray of sunlight slipped across its shell, going lower and lower into the depths of the coiling labyrinth, whirling in ever faster motion down the line of the spiral until it vanished at a point invisible to the human eye.

I didn't tell a soul about this loss. Anyway, the grown-ups had other things on their minds. The *Marshal Zhukov* had been taken out on the bay, and during the test run its crankshaft cracked. My father went back to work at his drawing board, and my mother started straightening things in drawers and cupboards as she always did when Grandma Maria announced her imminent arrival.

The sun melted the ice, and a strong wind from the sea, auguring autumn storms, dried up all the puddles in the neighborhood. I went for a stroll around the drain, which was visible at last in the September sunlight. I stared up at the church of the Resurrection Fathers, at the wooden belfry, and the red roofs of the houses. Then I began to scrape the clotted, crumbling sand from the cast-iron lid. Gradually letters began to appear, forming the words KANALISATION VON DANZIG. At last I could raise the lid and look down into the depths, but I didn't really need to any more.

Moving House

■ ■ ■

My father had hired Mr. Bieszke to come on Saturday, in the early afternoon, but Mr. Bieszke called it off. It turned out he had to attend a christening somewhere in the neighborhood of Kartuzy, so off he'd gone with his entire family and the move was postponed until Monday.

In the room upstairs, where we'd always lived, terrible things were going on: my mother was packing and repacking cardboard boxes and suitcases, and was cross at having to go on doing it for two more days; my father was cross because my mother was cross; and that meant they were cross with each other and with me in the bargain. I preferred to keep out of their way by spending most of my time in the garden. I can't remember if I was unhappy about that, and maybe I wasn't; until dinnertime I could do whatever I wanted. Only two things were forbidden: going beyond the garden gate into the park, and playing on the terrace, from where you could see through the French windows into the Great Room.

I knew the park well. Its greatest attractions

were flowerbeds grown wild, a weed-choked pond, a miniature waterfall that had been out of action for years, never spouting a single drop of water, and a stone plinth on which once upon a time, very long ago, had stood a statue of a king, or perhaps of a prince. In the dense undergrowth of nettles lay various objects: here a rusty bathtub with a large hole in it, there a crank handle for starting up an engine, over there a broken arm-chair, its upholstery disemboweled and its springs exposed. There were other bits of junk besides, whose purpose was obscure, or else forgotten. But that afternoon the park didn't tempt me, somehow. The terrace and the Great Room were quite another matter. Mysterious and ethereal things went on in there, to which neither my father nor Mr. Skiski, our upstairs neighbor, had access.

In the Great Room lived Madam Greta, the for-mer owner of the house. Mr. Skiski didn't seem to like the word "owner," because he always called her "the Heiress," cackling maliciously. My father simply called her Mrs. Hoffmann, but my mother always referred to her as "that old Kraut," which didn't sound too friendly. I very rarely saw her—she avoided us as much as pos-sible, and we avoided her.

"You're not to go there," my mother would warn. "She doesn't know Polish."

"Yes," my father would add, "there's no need to disturb her."

Although I didn't see Madam Greta often, I heard her every day. Almost every afternoon she'd sit at the grand piano and for two or three hours the house would resound with music.

"The Heiress is rattling the ivories again," Mr. Skiski would say dismissively.

"German music again," my mother would sigh.

"She's just playing," my father would shrug. "What's wrong with that?"

I liked her music. I especially liked it before going to sleep, when my father put out the light and shadows filled the room. Then the sounds of the grand piano would melt on the air, and I could almost feel their velvet touch; when she stopped playing, I felt sad, as if something was missing.

No, I had no desire at all to get to know Madam Greta. What would we have to talk about? All I wanted to know was what it was like inside the Great Room, and that meant getting in there one day, to watch her as she played.

I started walking around the house very slowly. First I passed the old maple tree wreathed in mistletoe, then the boarded-up windows of the outhouse, until at last I was on the terrace, facing the broad, glazed doors. Sometimes Madam Greta would open them and, standing or else sitting at a little wooden table, have a look at the garden. She'd gaze down at the stone wall, the shoots of wild vine and the flowering wisteria, and in the gentle sunlight her small gray head made me think of a startled bird. But that only happened in the summer. Now the doors were shut, and on the terrace paving, patterned like a chessboard, yellow leaves rustled beneath my shoes.

I pressed my forehead to the glass. There wasn't much light in the Great Room, and I couldn't see very well. The only thing visible was a table standing next to the French windows, entirely covered in objects. As soon as my eyes had grown accustomed to the dusky light, they began to explore this wilderness, picking out various shapes. There were brass and silver candlesticks, piles of fat books and scores, loose sheets of paper, china boxes and figurines, glass bottles, bits of dress material, needles and thread, earthenware pots, a pair of gloves, a child's toy rake, ladies' hats, cups with saucers and without, paperweights of lacquer and of bronze, a small bust of a man, a silver sugar bowl, some photographs set in frames, and an alarm clock with large bells, a little clapper, and one hand broken off. The contours of these objects were blurred and their shapes merged together as if seen through an out-of-focus lens. But what there was most of were

books and musical scores. Heaped up, they recalled a ruined city with ravine-like streets and
narrow passageways between one wall and the
next.

My initial curiosity satisfied, I stood there waiting for Madam Greta to appear, sit down at the
piano, and play. If she wasn't in the Great Room
she must be doing something in the kitchen, but
I couldn't see in there. The windows were too
high, and were covered with packing paper. Not
even any of the grown-ups had seen the kitchen.
Even on the rare occasions when they visited the
Great Room briefly, they never crossed the
threshold of the kitchen. The rest of her living
quarters—two sitting rooms, a bedroom, and
bathroom—were padlocked shut like the ones
upstairs, sealed by officials long ago. For as long
as I could remember they'd never been opened.
Their ceilings threatened to cave in. So Madam
Greta must be sitting in the kitchen.

If the French windows onto the terrace hadn't
been locked from the inside, I could have pushed
them slightly open, then slipped into the Great
Room. I could have had a good look at everything
and then left without anybody noticing. But what
if she caught me in the act? She'd think I was a
thief. While I was weighing up whether Mrs.
Hoffmann would complain to my father or not
and wondering what the German word for

"thief" sounded like, a light went on in the Great Room, and between the massive bed, the wardrobe, and the grand piano which loomed up suddenly out of the darkness, I caught sight of her diminutive, slightly stooping frame. She didn't go straight to the piano, as I'd thought she would. She placed a glass of tea on a small round table and sat down in a deep armchair beside it. Seconds later I felt a shiver up my spine. Something odd was going on in the Great Room, something I couldn't understand, and I don't mean just the German language.

As she sipped her tea, Madam Greta was talking to someone. It wasn't a monologue—she kept asking questions, making comments, shaking her head and gesticulating, maybe even arguing—a couple of times I heard her raise her voice. But who was she talking to? There was no one else in the Great Room. What normal person talks to thin air? I thought—perhaps she's mad. That wasn't impossible. I'd seen a mad woman once on Red Army Street; she spat at the passers-by and threatened them; she was all ragged and dirty, with spit hanging from her lips. Mrs. Hoffmann, by contrast, was wearing a brightly colored blouse fastened at the neck with an amber brooch, and a black skirt; her shortish gray hair bore the visible imprint of a hairdresser, though she didn't go anywhere in town except to the market at Oliwa and the Cistercian church. After a while, I found that by pressing my ear to the window I could catch a few words, and new doubts came to me: What if she's talking to someone she can see but I cannot? The conversation was clearly growing more animated—Mrs. Hoffmann was waving her hands about, explaining something heatedly, as if there was something the other person couldn't understand. Or was she just play-acting? But for whom? And why? I didn't know what to think. Yet the sight of this old woman, speaking whole sentences in an unfamiliar language, the sight of Madam Greta sitting in her armchair chatting to someone only she could see was so odd that I was rooted to the spot—I couldn't look away.

Suddenly the conversation stopped. Without switching off the light, Madam Greta went to the kitchen with her glass, then quickly came back and sat at the piano. I don't know how she noticed me; outside, dusk was falling, and the light from the chandelier was pretty strong. She rose swiftly from her stool, came over to the French windows and briskly opened them.

"Und vot arr you doink heer?" she asked.

"Me?" I tried to say something. "I was just coming by this way."

"Arr you hunkry?"

"No thanks, Ma'am."

"You vont zum tea? You do!" she answered for me. "You're to vait heer, gut?" And out she went into the kitchen.

Her steps echoed down the long corridor, and there I was in the Great Room, where I discovered lots of unusual things. The pictures, for example: all of them were very dark and very old; most showed horses, droshkies, and horse-drawn trams around the church of Our Lady, by Neptune's Fountain and beneath the Prison Tower. Or the grand piano: in its walnut paneling were ornate letters forming an inscription which I had trouble deciphering: GERHARD RICHTER UND SOHNEN, DAN- ZIG 1932. In the bookshelf stood row upon row of weighty tomes, the light gleaming across their gilded spines, but the stuffed birds—one white, the other fabulously colored—interested me more, along with a viper in a phial full of liquid. There was also a small collection of pipes and china pipestems with little pictures on them. Then my gaze fell on an open book which lay beside an empty vase. Two color illustrations depicted a woman and a man, but they were nothing like my mother and father. Instead of skin, or rather under the skin which wasn't there, there were swirling veins, entrails, arteries and joints, muscles and bones. They weren't exactly naked, and I didn't feel ashamed, but looking at them gave me a mixed feeling of curiosity and revulsion: if they were human beings, then I must look like that inside as well.

When Madam Greta came back, I shut the book; she set down a tray of tea, apple charlotte, and jam on the little table, and said, "Vee arr heving a Geburtstag. Zat iz a kind of zelebrashun. You undershtent?"

I answered that I did, and as I was eating a piece of charlotte she asked, "You like it ven I play, don't you?"

"Yes," I replied. "But how did you know that?"

"I kan zee it in your eyz!"

I was amazed. I'd never actually looked her straight in the eyes; I'd never even met her on the stairs or in the garden. As soon as she'd played the first chord, which rang out pure and strong across the Great Room, she turned around on her swiveling stool and asked, "Und vich tune do you like ze best?"

I didn't know what to answer. I didn't know any of the titles, and I wouldn't have been able to hum anything. All I could have said was, "Please play the good-night tune—the one I fall asleep so well to. Or the one you played when it was snowing, and my mother was standing by the window and called me over to come and watch the snowflakes slowly blanketing the park, the avenue, and garden. Or else the one I heard when my father was fixing the radio, which blended in with all the radio stations in the world." But most of all I was longing to hear the tune from an evening in June.

My father and mother were sure I was asleep. They were sitting in bed, covered by the sheets and drinking wine from slender glasses, laughing every now and then. When the bottle was empty, my father whistled gently down its hollow neck and they laughed again; the sound was like the horn of the transatlantic liner they'd planned to sail away on for their honeymoon, but they never had a honeymoon. That was the moment when the sounds of the piano began to drift in from the Great Room. Mrs. Hoffmann was playing a slow, sad tune. My father took my mother in his arms and they danced around the room on tiptoe, careful not to wake me. Through my half-closed eyelids I could see their whirling figures; I watched the white wings of the sheets as they slowly settled, until the light went out and I could no longer see anything, but the music went on wafting in through the open window of our room along with a strong scent of peonies from the garden.

"I don't know what it's called," I said at last. "You played it once, in the summer."

"Vell, all right. I'll play a bit, und you tell me ven you recognise it."

I nodded, and Mrs. Hoffmann began to play. Although it wasn't the tune from that night in June, I listened to it enraptured, and was sorry when it broke off as Madam Greta suddenly lifted her fingers from the keyboard.

"I kan zee zat's not ze vun you vonted. Do you know vot I voz playing just now?"

"No."

"*Tannhäuser*, ze overture."

"Tann-hoyzer?"

"Yes."

"Is that a composer?"

Madam Greta looked me in the eyes, then got up from the piano, took a book from the shelf and motioned me to bring up another stool. She opened the book at a picture of a castle: there were knights, fine ladies, minstrels, horses, banners, and turrets.

"Zat is ze castle of ze Landgraf of Thuringia," she said.

I turned the pages of the book as Mrs. Hoffmann explained each picture in turn, playing each successive movement of *Tannhäuser*.

When we were past the grotto of Venus, the duel of songs and Elisabeth's lament, and had reached the pilgrims and the wooden staff that burst into green shoots, Madam Greta said, as her fingers raced across the keys, "Now vatch out, here come ze trumpets, und now ze horns und oboes!" and I really could hear the trumpets, horns, and oboes, though the only sounds were from Gerhard Richter's grand piano.

"Is it all true?" I asked, once silence fell. "Did it really happen?"

Madam Greta took out a photograph album, and I saw pictures that were similar but a little different. On a large stage among beech trees stood men dressed in historical costumes, holding flaming torches in their hands.

"*Die Kunst*," she said, "zat's just art. Zey used to sing vot I've just been playing: *Beglück darf du nicht, O Heimat!* Zey vere performances in ze Wald— opera, you undershtent? At Zopott. Und here iz my huzband."

The photograph was of a tall man in a light striped suit, standing beside another man in a black suit against the background of a little waterfall and a pond. Both were smiling into the camera, and they looked like old friends.

"That's our park!" I said. "There's the waterfall, and there are the steps. You can even see the roof behind the trees!"

"Yes," said Mrs. Hoffmann, "zat voz ze park. Und my husband voz a musician und composer. Ze ozer man is Max. He came here zat time from Vienna to sing *Tannhäuser*. Both of zem are no longer living now. Und zis," she said, showing me another picture, "is Erikson. He voz a Nor-

vegian from Oslo, und ze season after he sang
Hagen in *Götterdämmerung*. Vot a vonderful voice he
had!"

"Where's Gerta Daymerung?" I asked. "Is it
somewhere in Sopot?"

At that, Madam Greta brought out another
book and showed me more pictures, then sat at
the piano again and played Siegfried's funeral
march, which sent shivers down my spine. Then
she played more—*Steuermann lass die Wacht*, and *Ge-
segnet soll Sie schreiten*, and *Wach auf, es nahet gen der
Tag*, until everything started to get mixed up in
my head. Parsifal was walking in the park by the
dried-up pond, Mrs. Hoffmann's husband was
chasing Hagen around the stage of the forest
opera at Sopot to the terrible wailing of the Val-
kyries and the Nibelungs, Erikson was standing
on Madam Greta's terrace, holding a flaming
torch and singing "*Beglück darf du nicht, O Heimat!*"
while the sailors from the *Flying Dutchman* were on
their way back from Oliwa on the road to Sopot,
singing "*Heil! der Gnade Wunder Heil!*"

It was all strange and entrancing and beautiful,
like the park in the old photograph. My cheeks
were flushed as I listened to Madam Greta play
on and on, a new piece every time, now without
telling the story, or showing pictures from the
books. We were both in an odd state, in a sort of
trance, perhaps, because we didn't hear my fath-

er's footsteps or notice him standing behind us. He, too, seemed enchanted by the music, or else by the scene in Mrs. Hoffmann's room: she stooping over the grand piano and I staring at her or at her fingers as if hypnotized. Or maybe he was bewitched by something else entirely. In any case, he stood behind us for several minutes before putting a hand on my shoulder and gently saying, "We've got to go now."

Mrs. Hoffmann struck a mighty, crowning chord, turned toward my father, and said, "Oh, Mr. Schiffbaumeister! Ve're just making a little music togezer. You're not angry, I hope?"

"No, I'm not angry," my father said, "but we really have to go now. Good night, Mrs. Hoffmann."

"*Guten Nacht*, gut night, gentlemen, gut night."

Once we were back in our room upstairs, my mother couldn't seem to calm down. Why had I gone there? She'd told me so many times! And what had she been doing to me, that old Kraut?

My father tried to stand up for me.

"She was playing him Wagner. That's all."

But an evil spirit had entered her.

"Germans! Germans! Germans!" Louder and louder she shrieked. "It's always those Germans!

Always building their highways and machinery. They've got the best planes in the world, and the best gas ovens for burning people up. Those Germans, they play Wagner, they always feel marvelous, they've always got hearty appetites!"

I'd never seen my mother in such a state before. She shrieked at my father, saying how pointless it was that he'd brought her to this city, how he'd only done it so she could spend five years living under the same roof as a German.

"Why didn't she leave? Why didn't she get out of here like the others?"

"Calm down," said my father. "The child shouldn't hear such things."

But the evil spirit wouldn't leave her alone.

"Why not? He's got to find out one day, hasn't he?"

She began to shout names, beloved names she knew well, spreading out one finger for each name, first on her left, then on her right hand; once the fingers were all outspread, she repeated the same thing many times in tears, for there were far more murdered people than fingers.

Unable to stand it any longer, my father asked her to stop, shouting at her that it wasn't he who'd caused the war, it wasn't he who'd moved the borders, it wasn't he who'd taken a city from one people and given it to another. I stood be-

tween them, torn in two. I could see their bodies;
I could see the man and woman in the color
illustration, like two pulsating, living wounds.

My father fell silent at last, then took some
medicine from the cupboard and gave it to my
mother with a glass of water. Finally she came to
her senses and made up with him, but in spite
of that, once we were all in bed, the word
"Germans" hovered in the room like a bird
aroused in the darkness.

On Monday morning Mr. Bieszke came. We
loaded all our worldly goods onto the cart and
the horses pricked up their ears, the way they
always do before the open road. At last we moved
off downhill, along the avenue, between the rows
of ancient trees. I looked back at the dried-up
pond, the waterfall that didn't spout a single drop
of water, and the nettles where objects of obscure
or forgotten purpose lay concealed. Mrs. Hoffmann's house grew smaller and smaller in the
distance, until it vanished among the trees, a
small brown speck with a red dot for a roof.
Hooves clattered on the flagstones; Mr. Bieszke's
horses snorted merrily, and he sang a Kashubian
song that must have been running through his
head ever since the christening: "I fancy me a tiny
drop, from this my darling little flask!" We passed the
bridge and the tram depot. The chestnut trees be-

gan at the top of St. Hubert's Street. The new
house, still unplastered, was not far away. Entering my room, I smelled fresh paint, lime, and
parquet flooring. Just then that tune came back to
me; Madam Greta had not got around to playing
it. It must have been a love song, but was it by
Richard Wagner? On the other side of the wall,
in the other room, they were moving furniture
around. I realized that I'd never find out now,
nor would I ever know who Mrs. Hoffmann was
talking to on the day of the Geburtstag, when I
spied on her through the French windows of the
Great Room.

Uncle Henryk

■ ■ ■

Uncle Henryk was a soldier in the Home Army and decorated after the Warsaw Uprising with a Virtuti Militari cross. When the same medal was awarded to Leonid Brezhnev for his outstanding contribution to the liberation of our motherland, Uncle Henryk resigned from the veterans' organization and wrote long letters to its board of directors. I don't know what he wrote, but I'd guess there was a lot of bitterness and anger in it. Yet in spite of losing the Uprising and the war, and in spite of a very hard life, Uncle Henryk conducted himself like an officer and a gentleman; I never heard him utter a single complaint about the material aspect of his existence or our country's political situation. He had his own philosophy, which I would now describe as the art of survival under extremely adverse conditions.

"A man must be strong," he'd say, "and there are only two sources of strength, my boy, the body and the soul."

Uncle Henryk didn't smoke; he kept fit by running and doing Swedish exercises, he went skiing and cycling, and went to Mass every Sunday and always took Communion. He was something like Cavalry Captain J. K. Blunt of South Carolina; Blunt was in the habit of saying, "*Je suis américain, catholique et gentilhomme,*" and Uncle Henryk had as much right to apply that famous phrase to himself, except he would have to have substituted *polonais* for *américain.* Of course, Captain Blunt was a fictional character who lived, as he put it, "by my sword." Uncle Henryk, on the other hand, was a man of flesh and blood who lived in an old brick house near the railway station and owned a small garden where he grew cherries, pears, and greengages. He certainly didn't have any cold steel blades or any other weapon, given the era he happened to live in. Despite that or maybe because of it, Uncle Henryk gave the impression that all the physical and spiritual exercises to which he so passionately devoted himself served a single purpose: to be prepared. At the age of forty-eight he was full of vigor and good cheer and ready to serve his country at the drop of a hat. I didn't think the need was ever likely to arise, but as I studied his athletic figure and the keen, bright expression in his eyes, I could easily imagine Uncle Henryk wearing the armband of the Uprising and giving orders in the thick of the battle defending our city's town hall. He was unusually cool-headed, taciturn, and swift to take action, the kind of man who from the very first word and gesture inspires total confidence in others. With such a leader, any soldier would have gone through fire.

Yet our relationship was strained. Although I sincerely admired him for his exploits during the Uprising, and although he was often kind to me, I preferred to keep my distance from him. I was never quite able to live up to his expectations, and things always came out wrong. When he brought me a set of dumbbells for my birthday and encouraged me to exercise, I lifted them no more than half a dozen times, and then, bored by the monotony of the activity, I put them away in a corner. On another occasion he presented me with some chest expanders so I could develop my arm muscles every morning and evening. This time it turned out there was no way I could manage even three pulls—I hardly made it to two, and I couldn't do those all the way. Uncle Henryk was disappointed.

"You lose heart too quickly," he said. "You won't get far like that."

I didn't know where exactly I was supposed to get by lifting dumbbells and stretching chest expanders, but it was clear that my puny frame and physical ineptitude grieved my uncle.

"You've got to be tough, my boy," he'd often say. "You've got to be prepared for hardship, but you can't even do a proper backbend or a decent handstand!"

Even worse was the outcome of my attempt at evolution on the horizontal bar he'd set up especially for me. After a few pull-ups, my chin reached the bar and I strained to turn but the metal pole slipped from my grasp and I fell on the grass like a heavy sack. Trees, earth, and sky all went spinning as Uncle Henryk muttered, "My God!" He stood over me, and in his gaze the hope was dwindling. Yet its flame did not entirely cease to burn in his soul; in spite of everything he didn't write me off as a weakling utterly lost to the world of real men. Our walking expeditions were proof of that.

Two or three times a year Uncle Henryk would plan a route, and we'd set off, fully equipped with compass, map, provisions, sleeping bags, and a whole mass of other things. Thanks to him, I came to know the buried corners of Kashubia, where the farmers burned oil lamps in the evenings, where they still used horse-powered mills and baked homemade bread, and where in a rough and raucous language they told stories of devilish tricks, of ghosts and vampires. The sweet scent of haymaking, the cool touch of water, the view of lakes scattered among the hills, the odor of nets hung out to dry, mounds concealing castles built by obscure princes, streams, rivers, for-

est mushrooms, pagan stones, and isolated
farms—it was a wonderful, real fairyland. We'd
tramp the length and breadth of it, stopping for
the night in barns or hayricks or beside a campfire
beneath the open sky. Uncle Henryk taught me
how to catch fish and use a compass, how to find
my way in a forest and kindle a fire without using
matches. In the evenings, when the stars came out
against the dark blue sky, he'd explain their
movements and point out the signs of the Zodiac.
We usually did over fifteen miles a day, but I
never complained about the weight of my pack
or about sweltering heat or rain, and Uncle Henryk appreciated that. One night, as we lay by the
campfire in our sleeping bags, listening to the
crackling of burning twigs and the lapping of
waves from the lakeside, he suddenly said, "All
right, my boy. In a couple of years I'll take you
to the Tatras."

I had never been to the Tatras, and the thought
that we would spend at least three weeks roaming
unfamiliar paths and tramping across mountain
ranges far greater and higher than the hills of Kashubia, hearing the roar of rocky torrents and seeing trout glittering in the sunlight, was like a
prize. I began to regret that I'd made so little
effort with the dumbbells and chest expanders
and had fallen so hopelessly from the horizontal
bar, for in my uncle's remark lay not just the

promise of an expedition to the south but also his acceptance of me. And that was worth a great deal.

But we never did go to the Tatras together. Two years changed a lot. By then I was in high school, and I'd been reading Rimbaud's *Lettre du voyant*; his poetry inspired ardent rebellion in my heart. I decided to become a poet and to die. If it had been for Poland, for the freedom of the nation—but no, I wanted to die as an accursed poet, a blasphemer, an outcast, abandoned and forgotten amid alcoholic fumes and clouds of tobacco smoke in some spit-soiled bar or shady hotel. The world of my childhood, a blend of First of May processions and pilgrimages to holy sites, seemed utterly repugnant. I smoked cigars, skipped school, and at night, with the help of candlelight and a bottle of wine, I wrote poems, so that they would remain after my death in a half-open desk drawer. My mother and father were sure that I'd gone mad and needed to be taken to the doctor.

"Take him to the doctor?" thundered Uncle Henryk. "Take him to the doctor! What he needs is a taste of the belt and some discipline. Look at his eyes. Is that the expression of a healthy adolescent? Those are the eyes of the habitual onanist. A young man should work at sports, he should take cold baths—he should toughen up. Yes, my

friends, he should toughen up, body and soul.
But what on earth is he up to? It's a year since
he's been to confession . . . Excuse me for saying
so," he said, throwing his arms out in a disap-
proving gesture, "but he has no respect!"

He didn't actually explain for whom or what
I lacked respect, but I clearly overheard the advice
he gave my parents. Keep him on a tight rein,
control his every step, study his every thought,
and that way you'll return your stray sheep to the
flock. But there was one thing my uncle failed to
predict: the next day I ran away from home, as
a result of which all his recommendations were
useless. When I came back a few days later like
the Prodigal Son, starving and exhausted, my father took me in his arms and said, tears in his
eyes, "Be a poet if you want. But go back to
school, please!"

Discipline, cold baths, and confession were
never mentioned again. I went back to my classes
and continued writing poetry, but I brought out
the cigars, fruit wine, and candles (which no poet
can do without) only when my parents went to
a concert or a film. If I didn't actually commit
suicide, it was because I wasn't fully satisfied with
my poetry. I tried, but my blasphemy and my
challenges to fate failed to have enough force and
novelty to make a sudden death original. And to
die without brilliance, to no effect, seemed to me

not a very happy idea. A few months later, in the spring, I think, Rimbaud sailed off into the distance. I stopped seeking him out and wrote no more poems. I also stopped desiring death.

The next few years don't really belong in this story. All there is to say is that Uncle Henryk simply vanished from my horizon; I only saw him now and then from a train window, bustling about in his garden, and once a year on my father's name day, when he came to present his compliments—buoyant and suntanned as ever, full of restraint and dignity. He didn't question me about my grades or sporting abilities. I was a high school student now, and I often went to the mountains on my own. Only occasionally did he cast a scrutinizing glance my way, and I felt he might still have a lot to reproach me with and still see me as that dubious boy, as if in all those years nothing had changed. I bore him no grudge for that. And the thought never occurred to me that one day I might set off with him again on an adventure.

But one winter night, or, to be precise, one December afternoon when dusk had fallen rapidly, Uncle Henryk rapped at our door unexpectedly. He was wearing a light padded jacket and ski pants (more or less the kind worn in the 1960s at Ornak), with a Finnish knapsack in a wicker frame on his back; in his hands he held skis and ski sticks strapped together, and his outfit was completed by a woolly Norwegian hat and some old-fashioned leather ski boots with square toecaps and crossover laces.

"There's fresh snow!" he bellowed from the threshold. "Why don't you come on a little jaunt, my boy?"

"What exactly do you mean by little?" I asked.

By now he was in the kitchen. He rubbed his hands together and asked for some hot tea as he spread out an army survey map.

"We could go this way," he said, his finger traveling from Hill 121 across Rocky Glen, down Birch Tree Walk, along Samborowo Valley, and over Głowica Hill all the way down to the old smithy. "This route has its advantages. But in view of the day's climatic conditions," he went on, his finger drawing a new circle, "we might also set off this way." This time the route passed the Swedish Weir on a downward run, then took a gentle slide toward Ewa's Valley; along Powder Vista it shot up close to the Devil's Stone and threaded its way in a wide arc through the hills to Jaworowo Valley in the Sopot district. From there, at just about the height of the Opera Forest, we'd gently bowl along to the first small streets where Secession villas and mansions lay drowning in deep cowls of snow. My uncle's finger came to a stop at the Sopot railway station. "The last train to Wrzeszcz," he said, glancing at a slip of paper he had ready, "is at zero-fifteen hours. So what do you say to that, my boy?"

"Fantastic, Uncle Henryk," I replied.

That was the start of our expedition.

We buckled on our skis at the edge of the woods, and then, after climbing strenuously up the road through snow-clad pine trees, spruces, and beeches, we could see the brightly lit ski slope with human figures skimming up and down.

"That chairlift reminds me of a tram," said Uncle Henryk. "A stop at one end and a stop at the other! Is that really skiing? Look at the way they do it!" he said. "Do you like that?"

We were standing at the summit. Spread out beneath us lay the slope and chairlift; beyond them, in the navy-blue darkness, the hills traced jagged lines, the lights of the city and the bay glittering between them. Tiny skiers went floating downhill in zigzags, then assembled at the bottom like ants, one after another, to glide slowly back uphill along the line of the lift.

"Can any of them perform a proper Christiani? Who knows how to do a Telemark?" my uncle said. "The classical style is dead and gone these days. They don't know how to do it. They're like penguins on a skating rink—that's not proper skiing. All they want is more, and faster! Come on, my boy." He turned to me. "Luckily we've got plenty of other hills to ourselves."

Down the dark, unlit slope we raced, stirring up clouds of fine powder that slowly settled behind us as if falling in a dream.

"Aaaand one!" cried Uncle Henryk, performing a Christiani. "Aaaand two!" He stabbed his stick into the snow and made a sharp turn. "Aaaand three!" He shot off of a little hummock and flew into the air, leaning his body forward for a good ten yards. "Aaand hup!" He stopped at the foot of the mountain with a fine, classic Telemark in a kneeling position, and millions of tiny white particles thrown up by his final swerve surrounded his silhouette, rendering him invisible for a second or so, then slowly floating earthward like a cloud with unexpected shapes emerging from it.

I rushed after him, straining to make out the path, but on the hummock where my uncle had performed his leap, my skis crossed and I tumbled chaotically into the soft snow and rolled head over heels several times.

"Nothing's wrong, is it?" asked my uncle, catching the ski which had run away from me. He leaned over me anxiously. "Are your legs all right?"

As I lay there in the powdery snow, gazing at the stars, I suddenly felt very odd; time, as if

coming full circle, had gone backward. I felt as
if I had just fallen from the horizontal bar in the
garden where cherries, pears, and greengages
grew, and my lips could taste the dust that used
to float over Wrzeszcz a dozen years ago. It was
the flavor of cobbled streets, gardens gone to
seed, well-worn footpaths, kippers wrapped in
oily newspaper, the smoke from locomotives, and
the grease on tramway switches; it was the flavor
of the dust from First of May processions, the
gymnasium, and the day of my First Communion, and I can no longer remember which of its
elements was stronger: the aroma of black cur-
rants from Uncle Henryk's garden or the smell of
the grease on tramway switches.

"You leaned forward too soon," he said, helping me to my feet. As I was strapping on my ski,
he demonstrated the correct jumping position.
"Just before the edge the body should be relaxed,
and in the next split second, you've got to con-
centrate all your strength—then you can be sure
the jump will come out right."

We moved on, down along Samborowo Valley.
The frost was hardening by the minute, the crum-
bly snow crunched beneath our skis, and clouds
of steam came gusting from our noses. Past a
great oak tree we turned to the right. I watched
the way Uncle Henryk flung his skis out ahead of
him and worked his arms, full of admiration for

his skill. If we ran a race to Oliwa or to Matemblewo, he would certainly get there faster than I
could. But he didn't impose too quick a pace, nor
for once did he mention the sporting spirit. Lying
ahead of us were a good many ascents and downward runs with about six miles of snow-bound
vistas between them. In the silence, I could hear
my own heartbeat, steady and rhythmical. On we
scudded, two slanting shadows. But what did I
really know about my Uncle Henryk?

All I knew was that during the Uprising he had
destroyed three German tanks and had been one
of the last to withdraw from the Old Town
through the sewers. During the same Uprising his
house had burned down with his entire family in
it, leaving him alone, like Job, on the smoldering
ashes; but unlike the man of Uz he had never
uttered a word of complaint.

What sort of reckoning might he have with
God? He hadn't lost his faith; he was religious to
a rare degree. As I shot along behind him in the
snow, that, too, aroused my admiration. To my
way of seeing it, he prayed to a God who invar-
iably humiliated the just and let scoundrels—
both with and without uniforms—dominate our
world. Perhaps Uncle Henryk's God was the God
of lost causes and lost wars, the God of those who
had been robbed of hope and freedom. But if that
was the case, then why was He known as a righ-

teous judge, why was He called Father, the epit-
ome of love and boundless mercy?

These questions kept going around in my head
as the snow flew about us like silver dust. It occurred to me that I would give a lot to overhear
my uncle talking to Him. He must have had a lot
to say to Him, and maybe he could even hear
something from that dreadful, unthinkable distance when he prayed in deep concentration, then
opened his mouth, daintily put out his tongue,
and received the holy wafer. But maybe Uncle
Henryk made his contact with God in a way no
one else could possibly comprehend.

Beyond Samborowo Valley the wind blew up
suddenly and a dense curtain of snowflakes fell
between us. We were forced to slow down and
call out to each other every dozen yards or so.
My uncle's shape would appear and disappear
amid the white whirlwind; he must have looked
like that during the Uprising, as houses, asphalt,
earth, and air went up in flames, and he disappeared into gusts of black smoke or acrid brick
dust, then re-emerged or suddenly sprang out to
fire at some sergeant from Munich or a Ukrainian
S.S. man. But whenever they got him in their
sights and let off a volley, he'd melt back into a
dense cloud and be invisible again as all the bul-
lets sent to kill him whistled through thin air,

because the walls of the houses of Warsaw had long since ceased to exist.

"If you like," I suddenly heard him say, "we could turn back. I wasn't expecting such a blizzard."

"We've got to go all the way!" I shouted against the wind. "Let's go on!"

He clapped me on the shoulder without another word. On we went, but it was getting harder and harder to make our way. The wind drove flocks of white cloud among the trees, and all the branches seemed about to come crashing down on us; to make matters worse, we could barely find the path to the Swedish Weir in the darkness.

"This way!" called out Uncle Henryk. "Left here at the crossroads!"

"Not left, right!" I shouted even louder. "Left is the way to the old ski jump!"

"What tree stump? The old tree stump?"

"Ski jump, Uncle! To the ski jump!" I yelled into his ear. "Not tree stump, ski jump!"

"Oh yes," he replied, "of course! But I think we've got to turn left to get to the Swedish Weir, my boy."

And thus for at least half an hour we wove a circuitous route, arguing at every crossroads. The temperature had plummeted below freezing, and the sharp wind cut right through us. We went around and around like souls condemned, unable to find either the Swedish Weir or the way back from it, or any road for that matter to lead us out of the woods.

"This is impossible!" shouted Uncle Henryk. "It has to be somewhere nearby, only a couple of steps away."

We kept finding places deceptively similar to the Swedish Weir, but every time the paths turned out to be different. Not one of them was sign-posted with the light blue route that led toward Echo Valley, or the yellow route to Sopot, or the black one to Matemblewo. At last, after we'd climbed a hill covered in beech trees, my uncle let out a yell of triumph.

"But yes, my boy. We've gone the wrong way. Do you know where we are? That mound is called Głowica. Hold the flashlight." From his knapsack he extracted a map which he tried to spread out on my back, but a mighty gust of wind ripped it from his hands, and the large sheet of paper floated off into the darkness.

"Never mind," said my uncle, putting his knapsack and gloves back on. "I've got it all now. If we go that way, we'll reach the path which comes out by the Schopenhauer mansion. But if we go that way," he said, turning forty-five degrees, "we'll get to Oliwa at the height of the abbey mills. What's your choice?"

I favored the path to the Schopenhauer mansion. It was only a short hop from there to the tram stop on Polanka Street.

"Right. Follow me, my boy!" cried my uncle, and off he leaped in a long downward run, maneuvering among the trees with astounding ease.

For some time we went along the gradually narrowing neck of the valley. I did know this road. On the left grew thick shrubbery, drowning in snow drifts, and on the right pines and spruces shot skyward along a steep slope. The gale was tossing the crowns of the trees, but here down below it was calmer. I stared hard at the first lights I saw, but as we came near the point where I should have seen the roof of the Schopenhauer mansion, or rather of the reformatory for juvenile offenders, as its function had been for many years, we turned out to be standing at the foot of yet another hill, even steeper and more forbidding than the last.

"That's strange," said Uncle Henryk. "This is where the passage through should be. A narrow gorge like this one—this is definitely the place, except that it seems to have changed a bit."

There was no alternative: we had to clamber our way uphill again. But when we reached the top, truly fed up and out of breath, instead of the Schopenhauer building fenced in with barbed wire our eyes were met by yet another valley, and beyond it an even higher crest of forest.

"Unbelievable!" cried Uncle Henryk. "We were here before, an hour ago! Well, it's pure luck that the wind has calmed down," he was quick to add. "Otherwise we'd be in real trouble."

I wasn't so sure that the place we had reached was the same as the one where we'd been standing an hour ago, that is, somewhere between Samborowo Valley and the Swedish Weir.

Then the wind lashed into the forest again with redoubled might. Bent toward the ground, we pushed ahead, groping our way almost blindly in a swirling white storm cloud in which black gaps appeared fleetingly, emptinesses without trees, threatening and indifferent. I was afraid that in an unguarded moment I would lose hold of the ski pole, the other end of which Uncle Henryk was holding, and fly off into the void like a helpless twig. It felt as if the snow storm was moving forward with us, as if someone above us was steering its course, and that everywhere else in the Oliwa woods silence reigned like a scene in a German painting, music still playing on the illuminated slope, and that all the merry skiers, ignorant of the rules of the classical style, were still going up and down, while we two, alone, descended lower and lower into darkness, as if down an endless ladder.

I thought I heard my uncle shouting something against the wind, and I was almost certain it was a verse from one of the Psalms, number fifty-five, in which David speaks of the white wings of a dove and how he longs to fly away on those wings and be at rest. But it must have been an illusion, I must have been wanting to hear the soothing words amid the raging blizzard and the whistling of the wind.

After a while I sensed that we weren't going steeply downhill any more, and suddenly a dark shape sprang up in front of us—a hut built of stout logs.

"We'll have to dig the door out!" shouted Uncle Henryk. "Otherwise they'll find us here in the spring."

It was no easy task. The woodsman's cabin, abandoned since autumn, was almost buried by the snowdrift, and the door, studded with heavy nails, was unwilling to give way. Once we'd taken our skis off, we kept steadily pushing against the joists, until at last, with a blast of wind we tumbled inside, with a great pile of snow, door and all, like a pair of drunken sailors.

"Are you there?" Uncle Henryk asked.

"Yes," I replied.

"Are you all right?"

"Yes. But it's awfully dark in here."

"Dark as the grave, my boy," said Uncle Henryk quietly. "You'll have to get used to it some day."

Above us the wind roared, battering the rafters, but inside the cabin, once we had bolted the door and kindled a small fire, it was quite cozy. The smell of burning wood mingled with the musty odor of the old rags and gauntlets lying in a corner. It reminded me of the aroma of the summer and autumn past, the bittersweet scent of bark, a blend of the flavors of various things and places: the loamy, moist earth of marshy ground, grasses in bloom on Luiza's Hill, and mint and clover from Abraham's Valley. And I thought to myself that it was this unique smell —of the beech forest and clearings bearing the strange names of princes like Subisław, Świętopełk, and Sambor, clearings which had welcomed Jan Sobieski and Frederick the Great, the smell of the trees that were silently looking down on us, a pair of ridiculous wanderers who had lost their way—that I would like to smell when I lay in my grave.

"What time is it?" asked Uncle Henryk.

I glanced at my watch and saw that it had stopped just before seven o'clock, which I knew had long since passed. But how long ago, if it really was all that long ago, I had no idea. Anyway, what did it matter if it was ten o'clock, twelve midnight, or two in the morning? I wondered why my watch had stopped. Had it got wet? Had I banged it against something? I had remembered to wind it, I knew that.

Meanwhile, my uncle prolonged his efforts to work out our bearings, even if we didn't know the time. He got out a traveling pencil with a metal cap and tried to trace our route on our sandwich wrappers. He listed aloud the climbs, turns, and crossroads, striving to reconstruct all the complicated meanders we must have made, but the greasy paper wouldn't take pencil marks. The trace of graphite kept disappearing, like ski tracks on a rutted path; each time this happened he impatiently licked the pencil tip, but when he went back to carry on with his chart, he had lost his place and had to start over again. Finally he crouched beside the fireplace and took out a compass, but when he brought its shining, nickel-plated face close to the flickering light, he cried out in amazement, "My God! Look, boy!"

The black and white dial appeared to have gone crazy. It was spinning first left then right, completing several revolutions each time and so quickly that it was impossible to distinguish the white from the black. The colors merged into a single shade, like the autumn mud on our streets.

In the monotonous voice of a lecturer, Uncle
Henryk started talking about the natural phenom-
enon of magnetic storms, the confusion of directions, and the rotation of poles. The time, for
example, when Halley's Comet came near our
planet, causing earthquakes, floods, volcanic
eruptions, and firestorms that raged across the sa-
vannah at the speed of wind. It wasn't quite clear
to me whether all these cataclysms were going to
come upon us, too, and if so, whether it was
about to happen at any moment or would take
place in some undefinable near future, but I
couldn't bring myself to interrupt him. Rattling
the compass, he said all in one breath that if the
sea had already surged beyond the shore and in-
undated Jelitkowo, Sopot, Brzeźno, Stogi, the
Lower and New Towns, not to mention Stare
Szkoty, Letniewo, and the New Port, if the water
had engulfed all the houses and their inhabitants,
then we were the only two people in the entire
city to have escaped with our lives!

"Wouldn't that be a true sign of Providence?"
asked Uncle Henryk. Without waiting for an answer, he expanded his idea: if such a terrible cataclysm were to happen this very night, and if we
were positioned at roughly one or two hundred
yards above sea level, then by dawn we might
turn out to be sitting on an island, two people
from a city which in a single moment had ceased

to exist, like Sodom and Gomorrah, Pompeii, Port Royal, and Lisbon. "Just the two of us . . ." he added after a while. "Do you realize what that means?"

I didn't understand exactly what he meant; I realized, however, that the thing he truly longed for—had been longing for every minute of his life—was the most extreme situation possible, in which he could cross swords with Destiny, face to face in open battle. There, at that moment, in a woodsman's cabin somewhere in the Oliwa forest between the Swedish Weir and Joanna Schopenhauer's house, for the first time in years, it seemed as though Destiny was favoring him by coming to meet the challenge.

I watched the whirling dial. It turned more slowly now, as if someone were wandering around outside the cabin with a powerful magnet. Uncle Henryk rapped on the glass face of the compass and shook his head again in disbelief.

"It's gone crazy. Absolutely crazy. Is it ever going to stop?"

"Uncle Henryk." I decided to try to say something. "Maybe we've hit upon iron? There could be a vein of ore beneath this mountain. Because a magnetic storm . . . you must admit . . . it isn't all that likely."

"A vein of ore? No, no, my boy, that's out of the question. The glacier left granite and basalt in this ground, nothing else. I've never heard of anyone finding deposits of iron ore in frontal moraine," he stated with a note of irony. "Unless the Germans buried a tank or some piece of ordnance here," he added immediately, "and we're sitting right on top of their rotten trash."

Yes, that was Uncle Henryk. Either it had to be a magnetic storm, the portent of cataclysm, or a German tank buried forty-odd years ago. Nothing prosaic could possibly come into the picture here—that would be far beneath his standards. The tools he used—a Swedish knife, an army survey map, an English compass, a Chinese thermos, even the metal cap that protected the point on his pencil—all had to be as infallible as he was; they had no right not to work properly. If all at once things slipped out of his control, it couldn't be caused by some ordinary hitch or accident—it had to be war, cataclysm, even the end of the world.

What on earth could I do? I fueled up the fire, hoping that before daybreak the wind would die down and we'd finally be able to get out of there.

Now that he'd latched onto the idea of the German tank, Uncle Henryk suddenly changed tack.

"They didn't bury weapons just to fight the Bolsheviks. They were planning to come back here. Adenauer, Bismarck, Frederick—they all shared the same dream, the dream of German unification. And every time that dream became a reality, every time the Germans woke up in a common homeland, it was always too late. Because as soon as the Germans get out of bed they're off on the march, and their marching makes the whole Earth tremble. You'll see," whispered Uncle Henryk, with an enigmatic nod, "they'll make peace with them one day."

"Who?" I asked. "With whom?"

In sentences swift as an allegro vivace and sometimes even an allegro furioso, in which the bugles of the Prussian hussars resounded and accordions and balalaikas rang out, he spoke of kisses in the air, of embraces that seize us from either side like surgical forceps performing an abortion. Various figures whirled through these sentences, all of them well known to me from postage stamps, photographs in schoolbooks, newspapers, and television: Stalin was dancing with Hitler, Adenauer with Khrushchev, Willy Brandt with Brezhnev, and Kohl with Gorbachev. As they drew apart and then drew close again, exchanging bows, my uncle spoke of a new border on the Vistula and of the city of his youth, divided into Eastern and Western halves. He said that on the left bank you would be able to buy beer and sausages and also gamble on a one-way ticket for the gas, while on the right you had to get a ration card for bread, salt, and vodka, and a work permit for some place far beyond the Arctic Circle.

"There'll have to be another conspiracy," he said even faster, "in both halves of the zone. Because the only people we can rely on are ourselves. The French won't die for Gdańsk, and the British won't die for Kraków. Only we, my boy, are capable of dying for a city we've never even laid eyes on."

He spread out his arms and went on talking like an inspired clairvoyant, and my eyes grew wider and wider until I wouldn't have been in the least surprised if those famous figures emerged out of the swirling snow and came into the cabin—Frederick in his wig and pigtail, Adolf wearing his armband, Joseph with his pipe, Helmut in his slightly too roomy suit, Mikhail with the blotch on his forehead, the remnant of a difficult childhood illness—brushing off their boots, then shaking hands with one another by the fireside and saying, "This is ours! Clear out of here, you Polish pigs, you misshapen spawn of Versailles! Out of our sight, you bastards of Potsdam, you scrofulous offspring of Yalta! Because if you don't . . ." But I was afraid to think any further, for what could we fight them with? A ski pole? A blazing wood chip? A woodsman's stinking, moldy glove?

"Does everything have to repeat itself?" I said, attempting to set up an opposition.

But my uncle's words and thoughts went on spinning faster than the compass dial and the snowflakes, revolving around the idea of a cycle in which great nations kept returning to kisses in the air and embraces, while the small ones that nobody wanted went up in flames or were transformed into an icy mountain of rags and frozen corpses.

Then silence. My uncle gazed into the fire and stopped talking entirely; I sat opposite, also saying nothing. I don't know what he was thinking about. Maybe he was waging the next uprising or stumbling in the white void, gradually turning into a snowflake borne upward by a gust of wind. I watched as the firewood burned, consoling myself with the thought that in the worst case we would go on sitting by the fire until morning, and when the sun rose and the wind died down, we'd find our path—and be amazed that it was so nearby.

Uncle Henryk dozed, resting his chin on his fists. We had enough wood, and there was still plenty of tea in the thermos.

I imagined that in the depths of the night, in a village not far, lights were burning quietly. I imagined silver spurs, cleaned with ashes and smeared with grease, glittering like Muslim moons. After all, we weren't in the Antilles or Provence. Snow was falling, and there were only a few days left till Christmas. In our city the red roofs of the Gothic churches looked beautiful capped in sparkling white snow, and if Thomas Mann were still alive, in that scene he would have found proof of the immortality of spiritual beauty, to which nature adds ever new charms. But my thoughts didn't stay on Thomas Mann long, or on the frosted towers of St. Nicholas's, St. Catherine's, the Church of the Blessed Virgin Mary or Peter and Paul's. The sight of Uncle Henryk's drooping eyelids and the glow of the fire flickering on his face reminded me of the trees in his garden, sprinkled with thousands of white flakes which cascaded down every time the express train flashed past the fence. I could imagine myself there, too, wandering among the trees, trying to catch a snowflake in my mouth. I stand on tiptoe with my head turned skyward, and as the last train, rumbling rhythmically, disappears behind the tall hoarding, I open my mouth wide and dodge in all directions. When one of the flakes falls into my mouth or settles on my lips, I delicately gather it in with my tongue and it tastes of unripe fruit—not sweet yet, just strangely sour.

I felt that that boy beneath the tree by the red-brick house was a completely different person from me. I couldn't equate the two images or merge them into one; it was as if in one of them I held a taut line and slowly moved upward in luminescent lamplight, while in the other I rushed downward, zigzagging headlong in darkness and raising clouds of white particles behind me like the express train to Kraków—the twelve-fifteen from Gdynia, the nineteen-twenty-five from Sopot or the nineteen-thirty-six from Wrzeszcz.

Would it have made sense to confide to my uncle that I thought I was someone else? If I woke him, he would wave me aside and say, "What nonsense!" How could A, at one and the same time, be B? To my uncle's mind our existence was unchanging and as reliable as the immortality of the soul.

I began thinking of roosters—the ones that crowed at dawn in the gardens of Wrzeszcz and Oliwa, in currant and gooseberry bushes, among bean poles and fruit trees, in wretched little hen-houses hurriedly knocked together, roofed in plywood and coated in tar paper, home for the roosters that had long since disappeared from our city, like the gas lamps, the horse-drawn carts, the summer tram line, the fire hydrants with cast-iron cap-chains, the shops with the remnants of glazed picture tiles, and the dry sand in streets and courtyards. Yet though all those things had

vanished into the past, the city was still the same,
as if it possessed a formula that nothing could
possibly disturb—neither fire nor bombardment
nor mass emigration nor, in their wake, a different language, different customs, different names
for ships and streets, different whispers and
pledges of love, different styles of jackets, dresses,
heels, and trousers. As I was wondering whether
there could be such a thing as the soul of a city,
Uncle Henryk started moving; he wheezed,
sighed, opened his eyes, and said, "I smell potatoes cooking. Does your nose tell you the same,
my boy?"

I couldn't smell anything like that, but before
I had time to say a word, he was roving about
the dark cabin with his head raised, flaring his
nostrils and drawing in deep gulps of air. Every
few seconds he stood petrified, like a pointer that
has caught the scent.

"Yes, there it is!" he gasped. "There's no mis-
taking it, my boy! That's the smell of potato skins,
hot and steaming. It can only mean one thing:
we're near human habitation!"

My uncle pulled his hat on, knotted his scarf,
threw on his knapsack at lightning speed and
knocked the cabin door open with a mighty kick.
A great cloud of snow crashed in and the wind
sent sparks flying through the room, while I hurried to put on my skis. At the sight of my uncle

vanishing into the darkness filled with the roaring wind, I had the horrifying thought that he'd been gripped by madness—the kind of madness my father had told me about, that killed a lot of people in those days, forty years ago, when all of a sudden in their sleep they thought they could smell smoked ham, boiled buckwheat, or— ecstasy!—pierogi stuffed with meat and mushrooms. With a shout they'd hurl themselves from their wooden bunks and run out of the barracks, and if they weren't shot by a slant-eyed Kalmuk for stepping outside the zone, they ran on and on into the white and empty void, until they ran out of breath, until the very last beat of their hearts was arrested by the kiss of frost. Their bodies were found the next day, sometimes not until the spring; sometimes not at all.

"Uncle Henryk, stop!" I shouted after him at the top of my lungs. "It's impossible! There's no village here!"

My words didn't reach him. Possessed by a single notion, he raced off on his skis, flinging his legs ahead of him in long strides, leaving me no alternative but to follow.

I don't know how long this extraordinary chase went on; all I can remember is that it covered several hills and I was at the limit of my strength when my uncle finally stopped at the mouth of a deep valley. Only then did I notice that the snow was no longer falling and the gale had stopped.

To our left was the dark silhouette of a village church; to our right loomed a cemetery wall.

"Strange," said Uncle Henryk. "It looks like a total ruin. Yet the village is inhabited."

At first I couldn't see a village anywhere, but as we walked through the broken doors into the church and looked up at a half-demolished ceiling, smashed benches, and the remains of stained-glass windows glinting in the starlight like jet beads on a dancer's velvet dress, I had a strange sensation, as if the people who'd got married, christened their children, and prayed here every Sunday had only left the place a few minutes ago.

"This is an Evangelical church," I heard my uncle say. "But why didn't the Catholics take it over? Why didn't they rebuild it, as everywhere else?"

The question went unanswered. As we passed the cemetery, I paused to inspect some arch-topped gravestones capped in snow, but Uncle Henryk quickened his pace. Moments later, already at the corner, he cried out, "Well! I was right, my boy. Just look!"

On either side of the road, a village lay before us. Brick and wooden cottages perched among the snowdrifts, with light seeping out of little windows and gray smoke escaping from chimneys up into the dark blue sky.

"Incredible!" muttered Uncle Henryk, as we came near the first buildings.

"Hey you!" I heard a shout behind us, in Kashubian. "This is Fair Fields."

There stood a small man in a workman's padded jacket, rubber boots with a thick felt lining, and a hat with ear flaps like the ones worn by Soviet tank crews in films.

"What? What did you say?" shouted Uncle Henryk. "What's this village called?"

"Fair Fields," the man repeated with a nice smile. "Or Schenfeld. You come with me," he went on to say, without waiting for any more questions. "You're lost, eh? Why wear yourselves out any more?"

"Fair Fields, Fair Fields . . ." Uncle Henryk kept on saying to me. "Have you ever heard of such a place in our region? I don't recall anything like that from any map."

Still smiling, the man led us to a farm; after we had entered a hallway and taken off our hats, goggles, and gloves, he bawled, "Hankaaa! We're eating!" Once in the kitchen, he said to us, "Have a seat."

We sat at the kitchen table.

"Oh Jesus!" sighed the mistress of the house, giving us a furtive look from behind her pots.

"Wandering around in such weather! Not fit for a dog let alone a man!" She, too, spoke only Kashubian.

"No more talk, woman!" said the man, and spat on the hearth, which gave a noisy sizzle. "Food, and make it quick!"

The woman shook a wooden spoon in front of his nose. "Don't spit on the floor! I said to you, didn't I, fool, that people might come, even in the worst weather, so I kept the potatoes and mushrooms on the stove."

"I'm not spitting on the floor," the man protested. "And don't talk so much!"

But the mistress of the house wasn't going to give up easily.

"You fool! Who was it who tore his hair and said they're not coming? And I said they'd come because I dreamed it on the first Sunday in Advent."

"What nonsense!" said the man, casting us a knowing look and tapping his forehead. "Like a fly buzzing!"

Uncle Henryk said nothing. But after we had eaten potatoes, crackling, and chunks of stewed meat in a thick sauce spiced with pepper, bay leaves, marjoram, mint, garlic, and ginger, as well as pickled cucumbers, marinated mushrooms, and bowls of raspberry compote, he asked, "Was someone expecting us?"

The woman dropped a pan lid, which rolled on the floor with a clatter. The man clenched his fists and stopped smiling.

"My name is Ignac," he said after a pause, "and this is my wife, Hanka . . ."

"Ignac," she interrupted, "give the gentlemen peace. Let them eat in peace."

"Yes," agreed the man, "let them." He stood up, threw on his padded jacket, and left the house.

We could hear his footsteps crunching in the distance.

"Ma'am, what are you and your husband hiding from us?" asked Uncle Henryk in a friendly way. "What's going on here?"

"Oh, we have trouble in the village and we were waiting for you."

"For us?!" we cried out together.

"For you or not for you. I don't know. Ignac went to the farmers, to tell them."

Uncle Henryk rubbed his forehead over his empty plate.

"All right, Ma'am," he said after a moment's thought. "In that case can you tell us how to get to town from here? Which way is it? We lost our way in the blizzard . . ."

"But why go back again right now?" asked Ignac's wife. "Why not rest yourselves a little? But as God wills it."

"Indeed!" my uncle agreed. "Do you have a bus stop here in the village?"

"Why shouldn't we?" the farmer's wife snapped, indignant. "By Depki's farm. We go to the city on the bus, but there's no bus coming now. The hour is too late."

"What line is it?"

"What line? The same as the ordinary line, the red one, the one that goes to town."

"But what number is the line?" my uncle pressed her.

"Sir, I'm a simple woman, in the war I went without learning!"

My uncle shook his head.

"Well, then," he said, "in that case we'll be going. Thank you for your hospitality."

But as he stood up from the table, Hanka ran to the door to block his way. At that moment a hubbub broke out in the yard, voices, and at least a dozen men lurched into the kitchen.

They started outshouting one another.

"That's them!"

"Where are they from? The city?"

"City folk!"

"And will they do? Will they do?"

"Ignac, hey, Ignac, talk to them!"

Ignac stepped forward.

"I am Ignac," he said, bowing. "And this is my wife, Hanka . . ." His voice stuck in his throat

and he couldn't stammer out another thing.
"Ignac..." he repeated, "Hanka. Hanka...
Ignac."

The peasants began to grow impatient. Uncle
Henryk stood with one hand on the table; the
other hung at his side, ready to make a swift
movement.

"What's the matter, gentlemen?" he asked
calmly.

The oldest farmer grabbed a stool and sat
down at the table. The gesture was a clear invi-
tation, and without a word my uncle followed
suit.

I watched the men's faces closely. Tired and
furrowed, they seemed bereft of all feeling, and
yet in the looks they furtively cast at us there were
signs of stress and anxiety.

"The judge cannot be from among us," explained the old farmer patiently. "And Fritz, who
lived by the forest, he died, a week ago it'll be,
may he rest in peace."

"Amen," the peasants said in chorus.

"And we decided that the first man to appear,
as long as he's not an official and has no relatives
here, must be the judge."

"That he must!" the peasants said.

"Are you officials?" the farmer asked us.

"No," replied my uncle.

"Have you got any relatives here?"

"No."

"Then they can judge!" said the delighted farmer. "They can be the judges!"

"Is it a matter of honor?" asked my uncle, still confused.

Making for the door, the peasants shouted out that it was one hell of a matter of honor and that if, God forbid, we refused them this favor, there could be real trouble.

"Let's get on with it, then!" said my uncle. "Let's not waste time!"

We left our backpacks and skis in the cottage. The men took us into the thick cloud of tobacco, sweat, and alcohol that enveloped them. Some were smoking hand-rolled cigarettes, others kept stopping behind for a moment to take swigs from a bottle.

"They may be armed . . ." I whispered to my uncle.

"No," he replied, "they don't look the type."

Not far beyond the village, at the edge of the forest, we stopped in front of an enormous barn.

"Mateusz!" shouted the peasants. "Mateusz! Open up! We're here!"

The gate groaned open, and Mateusz came into view, about to light an oil lamp. With his gray beard and long white hair, he looked like a saint in an icon.

"Praise God, they've come," he muttered,

lighting a succession of lamps which hung along the beams on iron hooks. "Praise to the Almighty!"

"For ever and ever," repeated the peasants. "For ever and ever, amen, Mateusz!"

The light formed an ever wider circle as more and more lamps burned with a flickering, golden flame. At the center of the earthen floor a small arena was revealed, strewn with sand. Around it were wooden benches and a single chair, upholstered in plush.

"It looks like a village circus," whispered Uncle Henryk. "In any case, my boy, be prepared. Above all, be prepared."

We were given no chance to talk further. Out of a dark corner Mateusz brought a second cane-bottomed chair, and my uncle and I were seated next to each other. Unbuttoning their sheepskin coats and padded jackets, the peasants sat on the benches and the buzz of voices died down.

"You may smoke," Mateusz told us. "There's no hay in here."

"Just a moment, gentlemen," said Uncle Henryk, settling himself in his chair. "Perhaps we should have some sort of explanation first. What's it going to be? A fistfight? Cold steel? Pistols? If we've got to be judges, we need to know something about the contending sides. What's it about? A woman? A boundary? An unpaid debt?

And anyway, isn't it a little too cramped in here?"

The peasants burst out laughing. They slapped their thighs and clapped one another on the back, and the ones with bottles underneath their jackets pulled them out and with a quick tilt of the head took a swig.

"Ah-ha-haa!" they roared. "Oh, ho-hooo! He said that! He fancied that! What a philosopher!"

I could sense that Uncle Henryk was like a grenade with its pin pulled, ready to explode.

"Men, no need," said Ignac to calm them down. "I am Ignac, and these are the judges. Stop the laughing now!"

"So then, Ignac, laughing's not allowed?" retorted one young strapper, red in the face, and cast a wry look at Uncle Henryk.

My uncle caught this look, and I don't know what would have happened next if Mateusz had not reappeared in the circle of light as suddenly as he had vanished a short while earlier. At the sight of him, total silence fell.

In each hand he held a wicker cage. He set them down on the ground and took off their covers; when the roosters' little heads peeped out, a general cry of joy burst forth.

"Oh, Isia, Kasia, Bernatka, there's going to be a slaughter!" shouted Ignac, or maybe it wasn't Ignac.

"These peasants appear to have lost their minds," my uncle whispered.

As a couple of men were opening the cages and getting the birds out, Mateusz came over to us, bowed politely, and said, "Your honors! The battle about to begin has strict and absolute rules. Whichever bird falls lifeless before the time is up has lost. But if an hour goes by and both are still alive, the judgment is yours. Whichever one has more feathers, whichever is the stronger, whichever has lost less blood, that one is the victor. Whatever you say is sacred, but you must speak justly. With this watch, honored sirs, measure out the time most precisely and accurately."

Accepting a watch in a silver case from Mateusz, Uncle Henryk raised an eyebrow and gulped. His Adam's apple made a fast and violent movement. The fine, long chain hung from his fingers like a pendulum, and I noticed that the hands showed four minutes to eleven. Meanwhile Mateusz walked the length of the barn, turning up the wicks of the oil lamps to brighten the light; then he stood in the middle of the sand-strewn ring, clapped his hands together and declaimed in a singsong voice:

> *Close the hatches of the corn bin,*
> *Come and gather round the barn!*
> *Let this battle now cast judgment,*

'Fore the time of year is gone,
Who's to hearken, who's to govern,
Who's slow-witted, who's the wise,
Till the feast of winter's coming,
Peace for all men be the prize.
In God's name let us now begin,
In God's name cease our dallying!

At the sound of such genuine folk poetry Uncle Henryk's eyebrow rose still higher, but there was no time for us to exchange views on pastoral rhyme and the origins of folk song. As the enraged birds charged at each other, the peasants bellowed with such force that the walls shuddered, and my heart was shuddering, too.

Never had I imagined cock fighting to be like this. The birds were nothing like boxers, who dance around each other for the first few seconds, sizing up each other's abilities; they were more like Russian muzhiks, who down a glass of vodka before moving into battle to win or die. The roosters were locked together, hammering away blindly with their beaks, raising a dense cloud of dust in the ring.

"Little rooster, give him hell!" roared the peasants on the left.

"That's a cock, no hog!" shouted the farmers on the right.

Uncle Henryk, grown deathly pale, was staring at the silver pocket watch. When the black and red rooster leaped on top of the brown and red one, as the terrible shrieking of the birds merged with the yelling of the peasants and the noise seemed to reach its zenith, he leaned over to me and said, "I can't stand the sight of blood. You know, my boy, this sort of fight was banned by Act of Parliament, in 1849 to be precise."

"But Uncle Henryk," I protested, "Poland didn't have a parliament in 1849."

"I'm talking about the British parliament," he answered irritably. "What did you think?"

Meanwhile, the black and red rooster had sunk its claws deep into the brown and red one; sitting on top of its opponent like a sack, it pecked at its head with all its might, trying to strike it in the eye and inflicting rapid blows to the scruff of its neck. Feathers flew into the air and dark blots of blood appeared on the sandy ring. It looked as if the final moment had come for the brown and red bird. Some of the men were already cheering, reaching for their bottles. Others were clenching their fists in silence or gnawing at their finger-nails. Then something extraordinary happened: the brown and red rooster turned around in a flash, freed itself from its opponent's grip, and struck him several blows in the belly. The black and red one was flung violently to the edge of the ring. It stood there pouring with blood and making a piteous wheezing sound.

"Go on!" the men shouted. "Give it to him! Give it to him now!" But the birds were worn out, and in spite of their keepers' prodding, the uproar, and the battle cries, they weren't eager to fight.

"Spurs!" they shouted from the benches. "Time for the spurs!"

I glanced at Uncle Henryk. His face had gone even paler and his lips were dry and chapped. The roosters were fitted with spurs, silver half-moons sparkling in the yellow circle of the lamp, and as they were dipping their heads forward and scratching in the sand, ready for battle once more, Uncle Henryk covered his eyes with his hand and quivered as if he'd been drinking vodka and it made him sick.

"Is something wrong?" I asked.

He shook his head, but he didn't look at the ring again; he stared at the face of the silver pocket watch, following the motion of the second hand.

A new spirit possessed the birds. Faster and faster they danced around each other, exchanging lightning blows and often clashing in midair. The spurs ripped feathers and tore off skin and bits of flesh. More and more blood splashed across the sand, and the men's continual roaring rumbled beneath the dark vault of the barn like a thunderstorm.

Uncle Henryk's mouth was trembling; his eyes, glued to the watch, were weirdly still. The fight went on for a good thirty minutes more. The black and red rooster lost half its comb and its left eye; the brown and red one was bleeding copiously and dragging its right leg. The peasants' faces were fiery red. The sharp smell of oil and the mens' breath was mixed with the smell of blood, strangely sweet and sickly. The silver spurs, covered with feathers and sand, no longer glittered.

At least ten more minutes passed. Again the roosters went for each other and collided in the air, but this time, instead of falling to the ground they soared up into the total darkness of the beams and rafters. Above our heads the spurs grated and feathers were flying; we heard a piercing "krik-kikirik," and then both birds, in a single two-headed, four-winged mass, tumbled to the sand, splattering blood in all directions.

The dull thud had barely sounded when Mateusz stepped into the ring, seized both roosters by the legs and held them up as a sign that both were dead.

Silence hung in the air. An instant later the peasants surrounded Mateusz, touching the roosters' heads, their bloodied wings, and bodies, hardly believing what had happened.

"Yours fell first," they said. "Ours was still living as it fell."

"Not true!" shouted others. "Yours was dead already in the air! Ours just took him up and died only after!"

All eyes turned to us.

Uncle Henryk gulped and wiped a fleck of blood from his cheek.

"Gentlemen," he said quietly, "they died at the exact same moment."

Before the peasants had time to utter a word of protest against this verdict, Uncle Henryk rose from his chair, put the silver watch in his pocket, took one pace toward the door, and fell full length on the ring.

I knelt down beside him and checked his pulse. It was definitely weak; luckily his heart was beating steadily.

Mateusz, who had also fallen to his knees beside my outstretched uncle, called out, "We must take him to the cottage! Hey, Kuba, Ignac, Walenty, get moving, look lively now!"

"Give him a drink!" someone shouted from the crowd.

Three men laid Uncle Henryk on a massive sheepskin rug and carried him from the barn. I went with them. The noisy, disorderly horde followed us in a kind of procession. At its head were the two dead cocks strung onto a long pole. Then came peasants with burning torches, while those bringing up the rear beat on sheets of metal, lids, and wooden rattles. The faces of women and children appeared in the cottage windows. Dogs started barking in the farmyards, and at the edge of the village a fire siren blared.

I thought of finding a doctor. Soon, however, Uncle Henryk had regained consciousness and, laid on a bed in Ignac's hut, was quickly recovering. Meanwhile I sat in the kitchen drinking moonshine with the peasants.

Over the first glass I heard how just after the war the Karpiuks arrived from beyond the river Bug and took over a couple of empty cottages, and how immediately a fight broke out. Nowadays no one can remember what it was about, but blood flowed—the Karpiuks killed Bieszek. In revenge the locals set fire to their cottage, and all the Karpiuks were roasted in the night like pigeons.

By the second glass, corpses were piled high, and fire and brimstone filled the village.

As I was knocking back the third glass, I heard how Mateusz came to the village. Although he was from the east, he was a holy man; he could cure people and animals with herbs, and it made no difference to him whether it was one of the Kashubians or someone from beyond the Bug.

I downed the fourth glass in one swallow. During this round, I heard how everyone in the village had gathered at Mateusz's summons and had done as he said, for how could they not obey a holy man? Ever since then roosters fought instead of people in Fair Fields, and whatever the quarrel, the person whose cock lost was the one who gave in. They'd sworn an oath that this would be a sort of divine judgment for them.

Over the fifth glass, the most celebrated roosters were remembered, but after the sixth, a gloom fell. What would happen now? Who would have to give in during the year to come? Never before had this happened—never before had two cocks fallen as one.

As I was drinking my seventh glass, the peasants sank into meditation and melancholy, for what was the use of talking? There hadn't been any real quarrels here for ages now. They waited all year long for the fight, keeping their best roosters for it and placing bets, and although it gave them a lot of fun and excitement, was it really enough?

"Someone's head'll have to be smashed in again," said Ignac, pouring an eighth glass.

I was about to drink when I heard my uncle's voice behind me.

"Gentlemen! This young man is in my charge. Please don't give him any more to drink, because he and I still have to get back home today." Into my ear he whispered, "I thought you'd shaken off your weaknesses. Let's be going, boy."

We put on our skis in front of Ignac's cottage, and the peasants pointed out the way: first straight along the valley, then left beside a massive rock, then turn across the wooden bridge, which you couldn't miss if you followed the stream.

The villagers' directions proved extremely accurate, which was an endless source of wonder to Uncle Henryk.

"It all makes sense," he kept repeating, as we passed each of the landmarks in turn. "It all makes perfect sense."

After that he fell silent. Not until we were standing on the brightly lit hill where the music was no longer playing and there were no longer any skiers to ignore the rules of the classical style, and the motionless chairlift resembled a tram line out of operation, not until then did Uncle Henryk, gazing at the faraway city lights between the snow-capped spruces and the Great Bear, say, "I never could stand the sight of blood. During the

Uprising I had to keep my eyes shut. You can't begin to imagine what it's like to run under fire with your eyes shut. So many times . . ."

We set off downhill, raising a cloud of snow as fine as gauze behind us.

That was how our nocturnal outing ended. But that's not how this story ends.

Five months later, one afternoon in mid-May, Uncle Henryk knocked at our door. He was wearing a shirt from an army surplus store, safari shorts, solid deep-tread rubber-soled shoes, and woollen socks turned down at the ankle.

"Be prepared!" I called. "Are we off on another little jaunt?"

But he was in no mood for joking.

"Those roosters won't let me sleep," he said. "Will you come with me?"

The weather was beautiful. We walked through beech glades, pine woods, and coppices; there was a scent of herbs and resin in the air and the birds were singing. Yet the idyllic atmosphere did nothing to improve my uncle's mood. He walked along in silence, glancing at the map from time to time.

We found the wooden bridge without much trouble. A mile further on, we found the huge rock which led to the valley where Fair Fields lay. But there wasn't a single trace of any building. In the spot where the barn ought to have been standing, a wild apple tree was growing—it hadn't been grafted or pruned for years.

"Maybe it was somewhere else . . ." I said.

Uncle Henryk brought some old maps and copies of even older maps out of his knapsack and showed me all his calculations and all the sketches he'd made over the past five months. He admitted that he'd already been here more than a dozen times and had explored the whole area, but hadn't come across Fair Fields anywhere, nor Schenfeld, for that matter.

I took a long hard look at a map from the Free City era, then at one stamped with the seal of the Prussian Land Registry Office; then I spent a long time comparing those two maps with the survey map issued by the Polish People's Army, stamped TOP SECRET. Over and over again I identified the spot where we were standing under the wild apple tree, and also the route of our skiing expedition. In the end, no less dumbfounded than my uncle, I had to admit he was right.

"Someone's been playing tricks on us," he said softly. "Or else there are a couple of madmen in this city—you and I."

We went down to the stream and sat on the grass; Uncle Henryk took some sandwiches, tomatoes, and the obligatory hard-boiled eggs out of his knapsack. We ate in silence, and when I decided to ask him what he thought about the inexplicable in history, or tales of the inexplicable, I noticed something extra in his hand: a pocket watch in a silver case.

"I forgot to give it back to him," said Uncle Henryk. "That's why I feel so uncomfortable. Do you think I should place an announcement in the papers?"

"Yes, you can always do that," I said.

A Miracle

■ ■ ■

The local nursery was called Ksawery's. People used to say, "I'm off to Ksawery's to pick up some tea roses," or, "They've got the best tomato seedlings at Ksawery's." In actual fact, however, there was no Ksawery. State Horticultural Center Number 17 was run by Beefy Handzo, who smelled of beer and sweat, had a leucoma in his left eye, and spoke with a dreadful accent, as if he'd just emerged from the mines to the surface of the garden plots in Upper Wrzeszcz. So why did everyone say, "I'm going to Ksawery's"?

No one has ever explained it. Perhaps, long ago, before there were any Prussian hussars' barracks or an Upper Wrzeszcz, someone called Ksawery lived there. I don't know, but I did hear that Handzo had been such a lackey to the Communists after the war that the underground passed a death sentence on him. That was why he fled Silesia and came to seek his fortune here on the coast, where the local Party Committee gave him a job as manager of the nursery.

I was extremely curious about Handzo. When-

ever I saw his belly overflowing from his flannel
shirt or bumped into him among the growing
frames as he shouted benevolently to the female
workers, I shivered. There was an indefinite yet
distinct aura of death hovering over him. If he
were to be found one morning riddled with bul-
lets (best in a hothouse full of flowers), my dim
daydreams, my secret longing for some real par-
tisans to show up in our city would have come
true. Sometimes in my sleep I'd hear a loud
squeal of tires and imagine a black Citroën braking on Reymont Street. Then three sullen-looking
men in leather jackets and knee boots would walk
up the narrow path between the pansy seedlings
and along the boxwood alleyways. Finally the
morning silence would be shattered by the rattle
of machine-gun fire and the crack of a pistol shot,
its echo resounding far. Handzo would fall onto
the soft earth among the orchids and perennials,
and the black Citroën would speed away toward
Brętowo, vanishing around a bend in the high-
way. But the years went by and Handzo went on
doing fine. The Communists shot a lot of parti-
sans, and many others were forced to surrender
their weapons, but the ones who managed to get
out of prison and come back from Siberia didn't
feel much like shooting any more.

Anyway, Handzo knew all about gardening
and especially about growing flowers. His roses,

cyclamens, peonies, irises, and carnations, his cinquefoils, chrysanthemums, and asters, and the orchids he grew in greenhouses, were all the most beautiful in town. Three times a year I would buy roses there, and each time I felt great joy at the thought that I'd soon go through the iron gate and between the long flowerbeds, that I'd wander among greenhouses from which a tropical scent of damp earth and plant stalks emanated, and I'd see pyramids of flowerpots with the workers in their blue overalls among them. Never have I seen women who were so happy at their work. They used to sing songs or tell jokes followed by a loud peal of laughter. They gave off a scent of vegetable tops, soil, cheap tobacco, and flowers, and this unusual combination of smells, which I could sense from a distance as I gazed at their crouching figures, their gingham headscarves and blue blouses flitting about in the sunlight, filled me with rapture. I was sorry my mother wasn't one of them—then I could have come here every day to be close to their warmth, which permeated my body and went spinning around and around inside it. But my mother didn't work at Ksawery's, and the only times I ever came here were before her name day, before my father's name day, and before the arrival of Grandpa Antoni, who came to see us once a year, usually in the last few days of August.

"Go to Ksawery's," Mama would say, "and buy five roses. Best of all Goldstars. But if the Goldstars have spots on their petals like last year," she pondered slowly, "be sure to ask for the America variety. You won't forget? Goldstars or Americas."

My father was fond of his father-in-law, but he found all these preparations and the atmosphere of a special occasion very irritating.

"Why go rushing off to buy roses?" He asked the same question every year. "Is Antoni a woman? No, Antoni is not a woman," he'd answer himself loudly, "and he's sure to think those flowers are absurd."

But Mama knew what she was doing. Whenever Grandpa Antoni came, it had to be as it was before the war: a white tablecloth and soup served from a porcelain tureen and not poured from a jug as on any other day. After the second course came the obligatory fruit drink, and dessert as well, and on the table in a crystal vase stood a bouquet of roses. Everything had to be just as in the past; for a short while the clock would turn back and there would be no reminder of the view that lay outside the windows of our apartment.

"What a performance!" my father would say. But even he could tell that the crystal vase, the roses, the porcelain tureen, and the silver teaspoons I'd spent the whole afternoon polishing were not really symbols of the past, but a challenge to the present. When I brought the roses from Ksawery's, Mama tenderly took hold of them, stroking the petals against her cheek, and arranged them in the vase one by one. It was a moment of happiness for her: she had everything ready, the living room was bright with sunlight, and we were about to go to the station to pick up Grandpa Antoni.

He'd appear on the platform with his leather suitcase, wearing an unbuttoned trenchcoat and a hat at a slightly jaunty angle, coming toward us enveloped in an odor of coal fumes and locomotive steam. Amid the shouted greetings of travelers, the crash of doors closing, and the rumble of mail trolleys we'd hear his voice: "So, my darlings, how's life in this godforsaken Hanseatic city?"

That year, however, when everyone was talking about Handzo's illness and saying he wouldn't last much longer, Grandpa Antoni gave us a surprise by sending a telegram that read: FLYING FROM KRAKOW STOP BE AT AIRPORT MONDAY STOP LOVE ANTONI STOP.

"Why isn't he coming by railway?" my mother wondered. "He always travels by train. What an extraordinary idea!"

"Everyone gets a little eccentric in old age," my father said. "What's wrong with that?"

But she wasn't listening. Hunched over the printed form, she read the message several times, and her expression was worried as well as disbelieving. Even the roses I brought from Ksawery's on Monday morning, with purple petals and droplets of dew on their stems, could do nothing to change it. Mama didn't like new situations, startling changes of plan, and unexpected telegrams. They never brought any good, and to her mind they always foreshadowed trouble. We took the number 2 from Victory Avenue, then the 4 from the Philharmonic building along Karl Marx Avenue, and finally the 7 which dragged itself relentlessly up Feliks Dzierżyński Street, and when we reached the tramway loop near Gedania Stadium, her face was pale as if the sequence of tram numbers contained some unsettling significance. Soon we were standing outside the airport terminal, looking at the light aircraft and some old biplanes by the hangars. A slight breath of wind stole into the air and ruffled my mother's hair as an announcement came over the loudspeaker that the plane from Kraków was delayed; an instinctive twitch ran across her face and I felt her touch my arm. But that was only the beginning.

A quarter of an hour later, there was a feeling of nervousness among the crowd of people waiting. The silver silhouette of an Ilyushin had not yet appeared in the clear blue sky, and the loud-speaker was silent.

"Why don't they say something?" fumed a lady in a black toque. "They should give us an explanation!"

"They don't know themselves what's happening," said a man with a dachshund on a leash. "Right, Josif?"

Josif barked merrily and wagged his tail as his owner expounded various hypotheses to the audience. Maybe the compass was broken. Or perhaps the chief pilot and navigator had fainted. Maybe they were forced to crash-land in Torun or Grudziądz because of a leaking fuel tank.

"Please don't go on!" a young man in glasses interrupted. "Let's go to the information desk."

Several people followed the bespectacled fellow to the terminal building. Mama did not budge. She stood with her hands on the metal barrier, its red and white stripes like a border post, and stared into the sky as if the airplane would appear in a moment or two. But the sky was empty. Meanwhile, the delegation came back from the terminal building; the information desk was closed.

"It's a scandal!" said the lady in the black toque. "Treating us like this!"

"Worse things used to happen in the war," the

man with the dachshund stated. "When I was dropping bombs on Hamburg, they got us right in the guts, my dear lady—we had to jump into the English Channel. Right, Josif?" The dog turned its head excitedly, but this time it didn't bark or twitch its tail. "Luckily we were fished out by a British submarine. I've sometimes thought they ought to have parachutes in passenger planes, because if a fire broke out, for instance . . . Or if both engines suddenly cut out . . . what would happen then?"

"They don't have parachutes?" said the lady in the black toque, suddenly terrified. "Is that really possible?"

Mama glanced up at the people who were talking. Her green eyes, which sometimes went brown, had taken on a shade of gray, as if ashes or autumn clouds were reflected in them.

"They've only got life jackets, in case of a splashdown," said the dog's owner. "But you can't have a splashdown over Warsaw or Bydgoszcz, can you?" The dachshund started yapping excitedly, the lady set her black toque straight on her head, and the young man took off his glasses and wiped them on his handkerchief. At that moment, somewhere on the torrid air of that August afternoon which rippled across the baking concrete, dry grass and arched hangars, we heard the distant but unmistakable sound of engines.

"There!" the young man cried. "It's coming from over there!"

Indeed, a moment later the silhouette of an airplane came into view. The Ilyushin's silver wings and fuselage gleamed in the sunlight like armor, and the low hum of the engines grew louder and louder.

The plane flew over some red-roofed houses and its shadow was already gliding down the runway when suddenly, just when it looked as if it was ready to land, the engines began to sound at a higher pitch, the pilot stepped on the gas and raised the rudder, and the silver Ilyushin, with Grandpa Antoni on board, went shooting past the airfield, gaining height until it topped the clump of trees in the cemetery at Zaspa and vanished over the sea.

The crowd went into an uproar. Several people ran back to the terminal building, while those who stayed at the barrier spoke in fragments.

"The rudder . . ."

"The steering . . ."

"The brakes . . ."

"A wing . . ."

"If it was the steering or a wing," said Josif's owner, "it would have been lying in pieces hours ago."

The lady in the black toque began to cry. Someone else began to whisper a prayer, but it was a stage whisper; every word of the "Hail Mary" was clearly audible in the baking air, after which a church-like silence reigned.

Suddenly the sound of engines could be heard again. The Ilyushin was on its way back from the bay. It reduced height rapidly and its fuselage rocked several times, but then it gave up on landing again and flew across the airfield as if tied to an invisible thread.

"The pilot must be drunk!" the young man shrieked. "A second more and he wouldn't have lifted the plane. What an imbecile."

"No, no," retorted the dachshund man. "It's just that he can't release the undercarriage. It's obvious, my friends."

"Oh my dear God!" cried the lady in the toque, wiping her eyes. "What do you mean, he can't release the undercarriage?"

"He can't lower the landing gear, madam. It's called a wheel blockage."

"So what's going to happen?"

"We'll see. At worst a belly landing. Without wheels."

"Without wheels? Oh my God!"

"It can happen. I once landed in Halifax, in a Lancaster that was heavy as a tank, and we had a similar problem."

"So what happened?"

Everyone fixed their eyes on Josif's owner.

"It was all right," he replied calmly, with satisfaction even. "The navigator broke three ribs, and the gunner cracked his head, right here on the forehead."

"Were you all right?"

"I had a few bruises. And then I got three weeks' leave in Scotland. Right, Josif?"

Josif barked merrily, and everyone burst out laughing. But the laughter didn't last longer than two wags of the dog's tail.

The R.A.F. veteran went on to explain that the pilot of the Ilyushin would have to keep flying until the fuel was used up ("There's nothing worse than hitting the runway with the belly of an aircraft when you've still got some fuel in your tank"), and as he was describing how the airplane would have to land "on its very last drops" without losing speed and without crashing into the ground at the final moment, Mama said, "Let's get away from here. I have to call your father."

The terminal building was rife with confusion. Pilots' white caps, dark blue uniforms, and gold buttons were flashing in the rays of the sun, stewardesses were nervously running from corner to corner, their heels clicking, and military men grouped by the bar were drinking soda water, wiping sweat from their faces and talking loudly.

Like a monotonous refrain the words "smash," "crash," and "hit" were frequently repeated, as well as "crush" and "slam."

Mama had no coins, so she went to the cash desk to change some money. As she stood there, and then as she dialed my father's number at the pay phone, I inspected her blue and white flowered dress, her white handbag, and the new sandals she'd put on for the first time that day. The slender straps embraced her ankles delicately, then ran from silver buckles down to her toes. I knew that all this had been chosen with Grandpa Antoni in mind; she always wanted to please him, she never told him her troubles, and she loved him very much.

The call went through and she shouted into the receiver, telling my father to leave work at once, take a taxi, and hurry to the airport at Wrzeszcz, repeating the same thing several times in an exasperated tone, because evidently my father couldn't understand if the plane had already crashed or was about to crash. As she passed the receiver from one hand to the other and tossed her head to flick back the hair that was falling across her forehead, I kept thinking about Grandpa Antoni and about parachutes, which—as the R.A.F. veteran had said—the silver Ilyushin didn't have on board. If only it did! If Grandpa

Antoni had a parachute, he'd be sure to order them to open the door and then he'd boldly leap out and glide like a bird above the city. I could see him flying toward us, getting bigger and bigger above our house on St. Hubert's Street; I could imagine the parachute canopy hanging in the branches of the chestnut trees. Grandpa Antoni would cut the straps with a pocket knife and jump to the ground. Or what if he landed at Ksawery's, in the middle of the nursery, somewhere between the rose field and the growing frames? He would instantly be surrounded by the women, each one offering him flowers, and though Handzo would start shouting that something was fishy, that he must be a spy dropped during the day by mistake, the women would laugh loudly and escort my grandfather to the iron gate. He'd come knocking at our door with a large bouquet of roses, the America variety, and say, "I've never had such a welcome!" Though he had never been a paratrooper, he had been a soldier, and when he was pursuing the tsarist and later the Bolshevik army, marching through villages and towns to kick Budyonny out of Poland, he was always surrounded by women who strewed flowers around him. In return, he'd salute them, because though not one of them was his wife or his fiancée, he was the sweetheart of

all the women as he went off to die for each and
every one of them on the field at Radzymin,
Lwów, or Warsaw.

Mama replaced the receiver, and we went back
out into the blazing August afternoon. The plane
had come back and was now skimming over the
roofs of Wrzeszcz.

"It's a Soviet make," said the young man in
glasses. "Once it gets jammed, that's it!" Before
he had time to go on, the Ilyushin descended
lower, and at some point above the railway tracks
the left undercarriage hatch came open; with it
came a wheel.

Everyone began to shout like mad, but their
joy was short-lived. The right hatch was still
stuck, while the left one and its extended wheel
refused to fold away again in spite of evident attempts by the pilot.

The roar of the engines grew louder and
louder. It looked as if the plane was coming in
to land again, and amid cries of "What's he
doing?" and "He'll kill them! He'll kill them!" I
heard my mother say, "No! Oh God, no!"

Then the pilot did something that defied the
laws of physics: he brought the plane down almost onto the runway and struck the protruding
wheel against the concrete surface. Then with a
macabre growl from the engines he raised the

Ilyushin back up into the air and flew off steadily toward the sea.

"My nerves can't stand it," said the lady in the black toque. "I just can't watch."

The snapped-off piece of undercarriage shot down the runway, the steel arm spitting sparks like an anvil, until finally the broad wheel broke off from its shaft and bounced onto the grass, then hit a hangar wall, which took the impact with a hollow thud.

The dachshund yelped wildly. Wailing ambulances were driving up from the direction of the city, and my mother, head raised, was following the silhouette of the airplane. Now that it had gained enough altitude, it was circling the airfield like a lazy beetle.

"But he had to do that!" Josif's owner was shouting. "He had to! Do you people realize what landing on one wheel would mean?"

The lady in the black toque grew faint, and the first ambulance crew got busy. Some medical attendants laid her on a stretcher, slammed the doors, and, siren blaring, rushed her off. Meanwhile more ambulances kept arriving, as well as gleaming red fire engines which drove onto the runway and drew up in battle formation down the side of the hangar. Firemen began unreeling long canvas hoses, sunlight glinting on their hel-

mets; from a distance the stretchers laid out on
the grass looked like deckchairs at a health resort
waiting for some happy patients.

Spectators from the city were arriving at the
barrier, including some newspaper reporters with
cameras. I kept thinking about Grandpa Antoni,
and about death. Is he very much afraid of it,
sitting up there watching all these preparations
through the window? Is he praying for a miracle
like the other passengers? Which was better: a
sudden death from a bullet or from an accident,
or a slow death which visits a sick man's bed day
by day and takes a little more life away with it.
It keeps coming back to take more, toying with
the man, tormenting him, until they close his
eyelids and light the final candle for him. Which
was better: dying in an airplane, unable to say
goodbye to any of your nearest and dearest, or
having to say goodbye to everyone in a hospital?

The plane went on spiraling above the city and
the airfield. For several weeks now Handzo had
been dying in his bed, crying out at night, "from
pain and fear," rumor had it, "between shots of
morphine." The moment of death was still far
ahead of him, out of view. He didn't know when
it would come upon him, and he must have been
feeling that in spite of everything he'd go on living. That feeling wouldn't leave him until the
very last, whereas up there in the sky Grandpa

Antoni, free of any pain or illness, was being led to his execution.

What could he be thinking of? Me? Mama? Plane travel? Of the fact that we're all doomed, and the only honorable way out is to make our own choice of the time and place of our death? Or maybe he was thinking about the roses cut for him this morning at Ksawery's, or the ones that had once saved his life.

When he returned to his city after the war and found a fiancée, he bought her a small bunch of roses with the last of his money and said, "Marry me—but first I'll build a house." Soon after that he met Rozenfeld, and they set up shop together, running a consignment warehouse and dabbling in the timber trade. Everybody warned him, "You'll fall flat on your face, Antoni!" but Grandpa just smiled, and every week he took his fiancée a bouquet with one more rose in it. Business was good and the house was almost finished. When the new furniture had been moved in, Grandpa Antoni took his fiancée a bouquet of sixty-seven roses and officially asked his future parents-in-law for their daughter's hand. Then they all sat down to tea, Viennese pastries and wine. Never once did he suspect, as he and his fiancée danced the waltz, the mazurka, and the polka, that his fate, fortune, and prosperity would soon crumble more easily than the Viennese pastries. That very

afternoon the great New York crash began; a few
days later the shock waves hit the stock exchanges
in London, Paris, and Berlin, flowing onward
ever faster, passing through Warsaw, until at last
they reached his town. A week before his wedding Grandpa Antoni had nothing left but five
suitcases stuffed with paper money. And it didn't
stop there—the banknotes kept multiplying at a
giddy rate. Soon there weren't enough suitcases
to hold them, or even enough trunks, until at last
the warehouse office was crammed with them
from floor to ceiling. Rozenfeld and his family
fled abroad, probably to Budapest, and on his
wedding day Grandpa Antoni was left with no
consignment warehouse, no house, and no new
furniture. All he had was dozens of drawers
stuffed with Polish marks—his own and Rozenfeld's. He could buy flowers with them, but not
bills of exchange. So he took the money to a gar-
dener, asked him to make up a fine bouquet of
roses in exchange for the lot of it, and after hurriedly jotting down a farewell note, he sent them
by courier to his fiancée. Then he went for one
last time to the house that had never been their
home. He touched the furniture fondly, stroking
the bannisters, upholstery, and walls. As he was
putting the barrel to his temple, sliding his fore-
finger across the cold trigger, he suddenly heard
a voice. "Antoni, for the fear of God! Is your life

worth less than paper money?" It was his fiancée. "How did you find me?" he asked, putting down the revolver. Then Grandma Irena—who wasn't a grandmother yet, or even a mother—fell into his arms and said in sobs that if he had sent the letter on its own, without the bouquet, she wouldn't have known where to look for him, but those roses, those beautiful Goldstars and Americas that he'd bought for several quadrillion Polish marks, had sent her straight here and told her to run on wings if she wanted to be in time for a wedding, not a funeral. And although they never had their own home or warehouse again, from then on Grandpa Antoni sold Elektrid radios made in Wilno, and every year on the anniversary of that day, in remembrance of his wedding and his rescue, he bought his wife a bouquet of roses, nothing but Goldstars and Americas.

Anyway, Grandpa Antoni might not be thinking of any of these things up there—perhaps he believed a miracle would save him again.

My father came forcing his way through the crowd, which had become denser. He was in quite a state: he'd had a hard time finding us. His face was grim, his brow furrowed, and his linen shirt was stained with sweat under his arms. He hugged my mother and held her close against him, and she burst into loud weeping.

"It won't work!" she kept saying. The plane

would crash. She wouldn't even be able to speak to her father. "We never took the boat to Hel together! There are so many things we never did," she said more and more softly.

My father stroked her head and gave no answer; in a situation like that it's better not to say anything. The plane went on circling overhead. When it went climbing laboriously upward it looked like a silver cross, and when it dropped or tipped sideways as it changed direction it became a shining question mark.

No, Grandpa Antoni wasn't thinking about death. More likely he was wondering what he'd have for dinner, or where he'd go for a walk the next day. Maybe to the pier at Sopot? Or perhaps to the Opera Forest? Or maybe to the old entrenchments and redoubts where we went every year to fly kites above the moats? From up there he could see it all perfectly, and I envied him that view. Imagine seeing the entire city and the bay as it appeared on the map! Imagine being able to see the ports, shipyards, churches, streets, hills, and the narrow strip of beach all at once, a view you could never get normally, not even from the top of St. Mary's tower. It struck me that Grandpa Antoni was a poet, a kind of artist, who had boarded the airplane with the sole aim of experiencing some extraordinary impressions of landing and then describing them in his memoirs. He didn't actually write anything except letters, but then he didn't really have to: I was his living memoir. On our walks in Green Valley or on Bukowa Hill he taught me far more than the names of birds and trees—he entrusted me with the past, which now lived only inside him, a past that probably no one knew as well as I did. The images of Grandpa Antoni's life were recorded in my memory, as on the pages of a heavy volume; it was enough to evoke a single one of them to set the rest in motion.

I could see the face of the German who stopped Grandma Irena, hit her on the head, took her bicycle and the food she'd gone to get in the countryside, and said, "You're a Jew! You've run away from the ghetto!" I could see my grandmother's face, standing there on that cart-track in the early afternoon, as the German military policeman unslung his gun and said, laughing, "Now I'm going to kill you!" Then I could see my grandfather's face, as she was telling him about it, safe and sound back home. I could even hear her voice, repeating over and over, "What if he had shot me? What if he had shot me?"

Overhead the plane completed another lap, and the flash of sunlight on its wing brought another flash to mind, the light bouncing off the river when Grandpa Antoni went fishing so Grandma Irena wouldn't have to go to the country any more and so no more Germans would grab her along the way. Grandpa stares intently at his float, squinting. He senses that nothing will come of it today, no fish soup or fried barbel, maybe just a couple of perch. His eyes are worried and sad, but not just because of the fish. Beyond the forest, long bursts of machine-gun fire rumble in the distance, and on the sandbank among the willows the hollow rattle echoes loudly, carried by the water. Grandpa Antoni knows what those bursts mean, and he can't understand what has happened to the world—it has lost its center of gravity, it's reeling and stumbling about like Jacob by the ford of Jabbok. On his way back to the city, his creel empty, Grandpa sometimes enters a deserted church, falls to his knees, and tries to pray, but no words of prayer will come into his head. He looks up at the image of God, despondent on the cross, and goes back home to Grandma Irena and my mother even sadder, and not just because his creel is empty.

As the plane was turning another gleaming circle, my instincts told me nothing bad would happen, for up there in that tin machine, sitting at his window, my grandfather was having the very same thoughts I was. And if we were both having the same thoughts—he up there in the sky and I down here on the ground—if both of us were turning to the very same page in the volume of his life and taking a careful look at it, we were bound to see one another again. Not up there, in the blue and empty void, but down here on the earth.

Once again I saw Grandpa Antoni by the river. There he was on the bank at dusk, pulling up his line, but the hooks were empty, so he cast it back again, then lit a small fire in the shade of a willow tree and sat warming his hands over it. He pulled the line out of the water a few more times and cast it back in again, because he hadn't caught a thing. A cool breeze wafted from the river, and just as he was thinking it was too bad for fish soup and too bad for times when owning an Elektrid radio, or any radio, was forbidden, as the twilight of July 1942 was falling over the marshy meadows, Grandpa Antoni saw the man. He was about thirty years old; he wore ragged gray clothing and looked as though he'd been hiding in the willows for a long time, or had come out of the forest. "You don't have anything to eat, do you?" the man asked. "No," replied my grandfather. Then it occurred to him that the man must be terribly hungry and might not have eaten for ten days or more. He reached into his bag and took out a stale roll, the day before yesterday's, which he'd kept for bait. Feeling ashamed, he said, "This is all I've got. Take it and eat it." The man smiled; shaking his head, he said quietly,

"Cast it on the right." Not until later did Grandpa Antoni realize that when the stranger said "on the right," he meant on the right side of the rock which protruded from the surface of the water. It was strange advice, but Grandpa took it. He baited the line and went back to his fire. The stranger reminded him of the handsome cantor Josele, the rabbi's son from Monasterzyska, though he didn't really resemble either the father or the son. Maybe he was just a ghost? No, he couldn't be. He was sitting now by the blazing embers and gazing at the water. His manner, like the advice he'd given, was strange and puzzling, but Grandpa didn't ask any questions, so they sat there in silence for some time. Then the man stood up and said, "Thank you," and when Grandpa asked what he was thanking him for and why he was off so soon, he answered curtly, "I must go," and vanished among the willows as quietly as he'd appeared. For a while Grandpa thought it was a dream, but it wasn't, for when he pulled up his line it almost snapped under the weight of fish.

The plane turned yet another circle, sunlight glinting off the metal fuselage as if off the scales of a fish. Mama was weeping in my father's embrace while he comforted her as best he could. The young man in glasses and the owner of the dog called Josif had disappeared in the crowd.

Finally an announcement came over the loud-
speaker that the landing would take place shortly.
Everyone was requested to please remain silent.
The medical attendants and firemen jumped into
their red-and-white vehicles and turned on their
motors, ready to drive onto the runway. Then I
remembered something else: my mother couldn't
stand fish. Almost every day until the end of the
war she'd eaten the zander, pike, roach, and eels
that Grandpa Antoni used to bring home by the
bucketful.

The Ilyushin was coming down to land. I stood
on tiptoe at the barrier, holding my breath. Mama
didn't want to look. My father held her head
against his breast as if she were a little girl. The
plane dropped lower and lower, until we heard
a dry crack, then something like a hollow whistle,
then another crack as if a gigantic sheet of canvas
had been ripped apart. At last there was a mighty
clang of metal and a grating sound which went
on for a very long time. Coming slightly off the
concrete runway, the plane plowed into the grass.
The fuselage was leaning on the left wing, which
had broken. Smoke was pouring from underneath.

The fire engines went first, and after them the
ambulances. Then we waited—only about two or
three minutes, but it seemed immeasurably
longer—until the firemen had doused the entire

fuselage in dense clouds of white foam, and from that great white snowdrift the passengers began to emerge through the rear doors of the plane. Among them we spotted Grandpa Antoni. In his unbuttoned trenchcoat and with his hat set crooked on his head as always, he came walking diagonally across the grass, taking no notice of all the commotion and the firemen's shouts. When he was halfway across, he noticed us and hurried over to the barrier.

"I'm seventy-three years old," he said, "and I'm very sorry that at my age I cause you trouble."

"That was a miracle," sobbed Mama, "that was a real miracle."

Two weeks later, as we were seeing Grandpa Antoni off at the railway station and he was regretting that he wouldn't be taking an Ilyushin 18 back from Gdańsk to Kraków, I remembered one more thing I still had to ask him. In that spot by the river, had he ever caught fish on the right side of the rock before? Before he met the Jew from the woods, I meant.

"Maybe not," he answered. "No, I don't remember."

"What Jew from the woods?" asked Mama, evidently alarmed, but the train had just pulled in. Grandpa Antoni got into the sleeping car and my father handed him his suitcase through the window. The conductor's whistle, a hiss of steam, and the roar of the engine drowned out Grandpa's final words as he said something more to me through the opening.

"What Jew were you talking about?" Mama asked again. "What's the story?"

"Oh, let him be," sighed my father. "Why can't they have their little secrets?"

Several days after Grandpa Antoni's departure, Handzo died in the hospital, "after great suffering," people said. He had refused the priest and didn't want the final sacraments, but his wife spoke to the parson, and on the quiet the parson sent a curate who, after the Party funeral, furtively said a prayer and sprinkled holy water on the cross she had had put up.

A month later I went to Ksawery's to fetch roses for my mother's name day, but they didn't have any Goldstars or Americas left. I bought some tea roses, and as I was walking between the greenhouses, past the growing frames and rows of boxwood, it occurred to me that the black Citroën would never turn up on Reymont Street now, and I would never ask Handzo if a sentence of death really had been hanging over him.

In Dublin's Fair City

■ ■ ■

"Holy Archangel Saint Michael, protect us in time of trial!" I'd heard those words before somewhere, once upon a time, but had it been in church? "Defend us against Satan's evil, O Prince of the Heavenly Host," the tall young priest went on.

People were approaching a small table in the east aisle. On it stood a glass case full of long, slender threepenny candles. I watched as each person carefully took a candle, dropped coins into a brass box, then went over and placed the candle in a circular holder. The candles made me think of the Russian church on Traugutt Street, set up in what used to be the German crematorium; the candles there were just the same, but Orthodox, while these burned with a Roman Catholic flame.

I wasn't in the mood to think of God or abandon myself to prayer—I'd come in here by accident, turning left out of Pearse Station instead of right, and although I wanted to get to Eden Quay on the far side of the river, I'd gone three, maybe five hundred paces in the opposite direction, down Westland Row, at dusk.

I'd left my map of the city on the local railway train, and it was now speeding off into the unknown as I sat staring at the empty, unlit choir stalls and wondering how I was going to get back to my hotel, or more to the point, how to find the way to the Liffey, where there was a bus stop on the right route.

The priest had finished his prayer; he genuflected before the altar, then disappeared into the sacristy, but there were no fewer people in the church than before. Some did leave, but new ones kept coming in their place. They, too, bought candles, lit them, and set them in the holder; they, too, kneeled at the pews and lost themselves in prayer. Bathed in a golden yellow glow, their cheeks, brows, and temples were like the faces of waxen figures. If they hadn't been moving, I might have thought I'd stumbled into Madame Tussaud's, which does a fair imitation of a church. But this was reality. The clink of coins dropping into the brass box was authentic, and so were the glow of the candles, the whispered prayers, and above all the odor of incense. That fragrance made me uneasy; it always had. Instead of thinking of Saint Wojciech murdered by the pagans in Prussia, or of Saint Stanislaw hacked to bits by King Boleslaw in Kraków, or of any other saint or all the saints at once, and begging them to intercede on my behalf, when I smelled incense I would half close my eyes, and the blinding whiteness of sand dunes would appear before me, with the green eye of the sea beyond, and in the sunlight I'd see honey-yellow lumps of amber. And now too I went through my ritual paces like the others, but it didn't have the usual effect. Perhaps I'd made a mistake. Or did they use something besides amber for the incense here? That's not possible, I thought, the smell's the same, quite distinctly Roman-Baltic-Catholic. My memory must have been deceiving me, so I decided to give it some exercise. Phone number? 680483. Address? 17 Pembroke Park. Proprietors? Mr. and Mrs. Brooks. Buses? 10, 46A, and 64A. When I'd whispered these words and figures, I reached into my pocket for the boarding house's business card, and there indeed, beneath the name ST. JUDE'S GUEST HOUSE, printed in gray, I read the same information. But I didn't give the incense a second try. I didn't close my eyes again and try to see the amber glow. As I was putting the card away, I noticed a man at the candle table putting a piece of paper into his pocket at the exact same time, as if he was copying me, or I him.

I watched his movements carefully. He lit a candle, set it in the holder, then sat down in a pew, but he didn't cross himself or pray. Instead he took a white card from his pocket, the same one he'd just put there. He meditated over it for some time, took out a pen, and noted something down. Then he put the card into an envelope marked with a black cross and went back to the little table.

Only then did I notice a small chest sitting in the shadow of the brass box. The man slid the envelope into it as if he were mailing a letter and wandered off. I noticed another thing—between the box and the chest was a pile of envelopes and cards. I went over to the aisle, picked up a card and envelope from the table and went back to my pew. "Dead List," I read with some amazement on the envelope with the black cross, "St. Andrew's, Westland Row," and below that in smaller type, "Names and Offerings." The card was self-explanatory. Beneath the heading "Altar Dead List" was a prayer in quotation marks: "Lord, remember our nearest and dearest, gone to Your eternity in the hope of a second coming." Below that, under the word "Parents," were two blank lines. The next five lines were dedicated to relatives and loved ones, then came ten more blank lines for friends. At the bottom of the card you were supposed to fill in your name and address; beneath that was printed the assurance that the parish priests would offer one mass daily for a month for all the dead named in the list.

Why did I immediately start thinking of my Grandfather Karol? Maybe those who have departed this life have a way of making their memory felt at moments like these, a way we are unaware of. In any case I started to think of him. There he is—not very tall, in a gray duster, stick in hand, measuring the length of the beach at a calm, even pace, deep in thought. Cumulus clouds swirl overhead and a shell crunches beneath his feet. The scuttling of a crab and the cawing of a raven are drowned in the roar of dark green, whitecapped waves.

That's how I pictured him after all these years, as I sat on a bench in the church in Westland Row, the dead list in my hands. I could taste the salt on my lips, infused with the bitter odor of algae and seaweed; it was in that same season of jellyfish and autumn winds that I saw him for the last time. I never suspected then that madness was consuming him, that sinister, scheming illness never spoken of in my presence after he had gone. I began to remember my father's lowered voice as he talked to my mother about it in the kitchen in the evenings. I'd strain to catch disjointed phrases such as, "She's the pastor's widow," or, "He's hidden himself away on

purpose," or else, "It's not easy to get there."
"Where is he?" I'd ask. "Is he in danger? Why
doesn't he go back to Kraków, where Grandma
Maria is waiting for him?" Whenever I asked
these questions my father, pale and upset, would
leave the room, and Mama would explain, "You're
too young to understand. One day the time will
come." But the time never did come, so over the
passing weeks and months I carefully thought
through everything my grandfather had said, everything he'd done during those two weeks in
October.

As we marched along the beach from Sopot to
Jelitkowo or back again, he'd want to stop and
stand over the jellyfish cast up on the shore. Delicately turning them over with the point of his
stick to examine the network of violet veins, he'd
say, "It's all over now. It's all over," or, "There
are no more houses left in ruins." I couldn't understand what he meant, but I didn't dare ask. He
wasn't speaking to me but to the jellyfish, or into
the air—to the waves and the wind and the
wheeling seagulls. Sometimes he stood immobile,
gazing out toward the bay at the bright blue line
of the horizon, as if expecting a sign to appear
there, or wanting to see something in the distance. If our walk ended in Sopot, sometimes
we'd drop in at Mr. Lipszyc's shop, located almost directly under the railway viaduct, where I

delighted in inspecting the music boxes and cuckoo clocks while Grandfather went into a back room. There, in the half-light of a feeble lamp, he and the watchmaker pored over maps that Mr. Lipszyc had acquired especially for him. They were navigational maps, mostly Swedish or German. "Thank you," said Grandfather, "I'd never manage without your help." Mr. Lipszyc would reply that if only he had more clients who wrote books about lighthouses, like Grandfather, he'd open an antiquarian shop. Grandfather put the maps into his coat pocket after folding them up carefully, which wasn't difficult since Mr. Lip-szyc had glued canvas to the back of the paper. As we were on the train back home, passing the racetrack, Oliwa, Polanka Street, and the airfield, Grandfather would stare out of the window and say nonchalantly, "It will be a surprise. Until I've actually written the book, please don't say a word to anyone."

I believed him. I believed him unconditionally. He was a chemist, had even patented a couple of inventions, but after the war he could never find a permanent job and earned his living erratically, working as a photographer's lab assistant or as a traveling salesman hawking fireworks and caps at fairs. Why shouldn't he find fame and fortune with a wonderful new book about lighthouses? I didn't find it strange. What was strange were our visits to Mr. Hamerling's, at the other end of town, where a one-story half-timbered house with a gabled roof stood among the canals. next to the Dutch lock.

Above the weir, dry leaves rustled underfoot. Our feet drummed across a little wooden bridge and creaked up a narrow staircase leading to the attic and the door of Mr. Gustaw Hamerling's apartment. Everything in there smelled of mint— the books Mr. Hamerling extracted from innumerable chests and trunks, the tobacco with which he stuffed his pipe, the tea he entertained us with, and even the scarf eternally wound around his neck, even that scarf smelled of mint, because everywhere under the roof beams and on the wooden walls small bags full of mint leaves were hanging. "It's sheer health," our host would say, pouring us mugs of mint tea. "It has a marvelous effect on the digestion and the nerves," he added, puffing minty smoke from his pipe. As we were drinking our tea, he offered us candy— mints, of course.

The two of them spoke in German, though each in a different way: Grandfather Karol softly and calmly, and Mr. Hamerling gutturally and emphatically. "It's to give us practice," Grandfather explained to me afterward, but I felt they wanted to hide something from me, something they clearly disagreed about but that at the same time tied them together by a strong bond. As they chatted, frequently reaching for books full of technical drawings, I wandered around the room or went to the window, from where I could see old fortifications, a moat, the Motława canal, and the lock which had been out of operation for many years. "*Warum?*" asked Grandfather. "*Darum*," replied Mr. Hamerling. "*Möglich*," said Grandfather. "*Unmöglich!*" Mr. Hamerling countered. That was how it went throughout their conversation, which, apart from a couple of phrases, I didn't understand. They were arguing about a question of great interest to both of them, to which Mr. Hamerling's books, which they leafed through so feverishly, gave no straight answer. Furtively glancing at the pages, I saw columns of figures, diagrams of tubing and connections. "*Muss es sein?*" asked Grandfather at one point. "*Es muss sein!*" retorted Mr. Hamerling. "*Es muss sein, mein liebe doktor Karol! Es muss sein!*" It was their final conversation. As they were bidding each other farewell downstairs, in Polish now, Mr. Hamerling said, "Just be sure to watch your blood pressure!" "I will indeed," replied Grandfather. "I'll keep drinking the mint tea, morning, noon, and night."

"Is anything the matter? Aren't you feeling well?" The voice was not Grandfather Karol's or Mr. Hamerling's. By now the candles had burned out in their holder, wax was dripping onto the floor, and before me stood the priest who had conducted the service earlier. We were alone in the church, and the electric lights had been switched off.

"No, thanks," I answered quietly. "Everything's fine."

"Oh, you're a foreigner. I see!" he said with evident pleasure. "Would you like me to hear your confession?"

The question was so sudden and unexpected, and his face so full of benevolence, that I quite forgot myself and answered in Polish, "No, thank you very much, Father."

"Oh!" he said, raising his hands. "Are you Russian?"

He didn't notice the card and envelope; I'd managed to hide them in my pocket. I got up from the pew and moved toward the exit, replying that no, I wasn't Russian, which seemed to disappoint him. He followed me all the way to the door and asked if he could help me in any way, asked where I came from, asked whether I was a tourist or perhaps an émigré.

"Thanks," I repeated, already in the doorway. "Everything's fine. I'm visiting the city and I lost my map. Could you please tell me, Father, how to get to Eden Quay?"

As he told me, I studied his face. It was intel-

ligent, as yet untouched by the sins of doubt or
despair. He looked as if he could have worked
with drug addicts, reformed drunkards, or spread
the Good News to prostitutes and criminals.

"Thank you," I said, as he offered me his hand.
"Now I'll be all right."

"But where are you from?" he persisted. "I
thought what you said, that sentence, I thought
it was in Russian." When I mentioned the name,
he looked perplexed and asked, "Where's that? Is
it somewhere in the East?"

"In a way," I replied after a moment's hesita-
tion. "But it's an unreal city . . . I must be going
now. Excuse me. Goodbye."

"Goodbye. May God be with you," I heard his
voice, by now at a distance of several stone steps
above me. From the corner of my eye I saw him
discreetly blessing me with the sign of the cross.
Or perhaps it wasn't me he was blessing but my
unreal city.

I decided to walk to Pearse Station and catch a
taxi there. Not for fear of getting lost—I was on
the right road now—but I could feel the chill; an
unpleasant mist was rising in the air and it didn't
inspire me to walk any farther. Besides, I was
bothered by the thought, or rather the question,
of whether I ought to go back to the church and
order a mass for the soul of Grandfather Karol.
Perhaps I should pray for him. His soul, wherever

it was, whether in Sheol, the Elysian Fields, by the waters of the Styx, or in Valhalla, was surely suffering as much as it had in his body. I felt helpless, lost among these guesses and suppositions, for what word, what spell, what incantation or song could I conjure up to soothe that soul? What prayer could I say to persuade God to grant it peace and eternal redemption? What if Martin Luther was right when he said that our deeds are quite useless and saying prayers for the dead is pointless, that only destiny is real?

These weren't the best thoughts for a walk in a foreign city, especially at dusk. Quite near Pearse Station, I decided to cross the road and start looking for a taxi, when suddenly, still on the same side of Westland Row, I was accosted by a tramp.

"You!" he shouted. "What do you think of Saint Columba?"

"Nothing," I replied, "nothing at all."

He wasn't discouraged by my answer, but played a couple of bars on his violin, then started singing hoarsely:

> O won't we have a merry time
> Drinking whiskey, beer and wine
> On Samhain,
> Samhain day?

Between his feet was a box similar to the one in the church, but with a wider coin slot. As he played, he kicked it in time to the music, as if in accompaniment. I took out a six-sided coin with the coat of arms of the city on one side and a stylized lyre on the other. The money made a solid clattering sound, first merrily, then mournfully, as the singer repeated the last two lines

> On Samhain,
> Samhain day?

and said, "Because what I say, brother, what I say is, Saint Columba be damned. And all the other saints as well. But not Patrick—Patrick's something else, Patrick is you and me, he's every one of us, all the brothers and sisters of this devilish emerald mother of ours. Eh?"

I walked away with no regret for the coin with this city's coats of arms; he started singing something else, but I could no longer hear him. Again I was beset by the idea that I ought to go back to the church and put my grandfather's name down on the dead list to order a mass for him. This thought wouldn't leave me alone, however hard I tried to push it away.

The short letters that Grandma Maria kept sending to my father must have been dramatic, for one day in spring he took two days' leave and went off by train to a place beyond Olsztyn, in

Eastern Prussia. He came back with a serious look on his face, extremely dejected, as if there was a burden of fate on his shoulders that far exceeded his strength. "I just cannot accept it! I cannot understand it!" he said again and again. He shut himself in the kitchen with Mama, and I overheard him telling her that it had nothing at all to do with a woman, least of all the pastor's widow, as Grandma Maria imagined. It was something else entirely, a sort of insanity, in which he'd locked himself away, as if in a tower patrolled by ghosts, and there he stayed, silent and indifferent to the appeals of his loved ones. "There is some method in it, though," said my father. "Do you know what he reads all the time?" He mentioned a Latin title I couldn't understand.

If I'd told my father then about our visits to Mr. Lipszyc or particularly to Mr. Hamerling, might I have saved my grandfather? As I was pondering this question, I looked left out of habit and crossed the road diagonally. Probably not, I was thinking, when I heard a squeal of tires and loud honking and felt a strangely gentle blow to my right side. Luckily the delivery van, an old green Ford, had slowed down in time, and as I was picking myself up from the road I felt nothing but a small, sharp pain in my knee. A girl in a thick sweater leaped from the van. She was about twenty-five, maybe a little older.

"Hey!" she shouted. "Are you drunk? Are you blind?" She was more upset than I was and couldn't stop her hands from shaking. She kept tossing her head, flinging back the chestnut hair that fell across her forehead in rippling bangs. "You're all the same," she said, a little calmer now. "A couple of quick ones in the pub, then straight under the wheels of a car. Do we have to go to the hospital?"

I began dusting off my coat and trousers, looking into her dark green eyes, which waited for an answer.

"Why don't you say something? Lost for words, are you?"

"Yes," I replied. "First you bump me in the backside and now you shout at me."

"How funny he talks!" she cried. "I bump him in the backside and now I shout at him." She mimicked my accent.

Both of us burst out laughing. A couple of gawking passers-by gave up and went away—it wasn't a serious accident after all. I said I was quite all right and there was no need for the hospital.

"Are you a tourist?" she asked.

I didn't deny it, and added that the next day I was off to Galway by bus.

She offered her hand. Her fingers were long and cold as ice.

"When you cross the street, first look right,"
she said, getting back into the van. "This is a
weird country, where the cars drive on the left."

"Yes, it's a weird country," I replied.

But she was already out of earshot. The delivery van which bore the legend LIVE COCKLES AND
MUSSELS was on its way, gear box grating. I set off
again for Pearse Station, which I seemed to be
having trouble reaching.

"Must you haunt me?" I said under my breath.
"Didn't my lips whisper enough prayers in the
church of the Resurrection Fathers? Don't you remember how I used to leap out of bed at dawn
and run to the earliest mass without any breakfast, on nothing but a glass of water? I prayed
fervently, passionately, feverishly for your recovery, for your return, for your happiness; then I
received His body from the hand of the priest,
and I swallowed it for you alone in all the world.
I'd go home for my satchel and run to school,
but I never stopped thinking about you, never for
a moment, just as now, not even when the peasant carts came rumbling by on their way to the
Oliwa market. Not even the horses' snorting or
the clip-clop of their hooves could disturb my
constant prayer offered up for you and for myself.
And now? I can't help you any more, not in any
way. Forgive me. Even if it was no accident that
took me into that church, even if it was your

doing, please stop following me! This is not your
city—all that's left of your city is a dream. It was
betrayed and sold off long ago; perhaps some
trees, walls, and cemeteries remain, perhaps the
bench you used to sit on is still there in the park,
perhaps the same dust still lies on the streets in
August—what can I tell you, what can I still do
for you? Should I recite all those names that mean
nothing more to me than empty sounds? The
domes of St. Bernard's in the first snow, the jingle
of harnesses in Łyczaków, the gentle breath of the
Carpathians blowing from behind, the sound of
a Ukrainian song? . . . Forget it all, forget it! Those
swirling atoms will never return to their former
state, and all my promises are futile . . . Do you
understand me? Do you hear me? I'm not going
to make any more fruitless appeals."

I don't know where my rush of words and
steps would have led me if my leg hadn't started
aching sharply. "So where is Pearse Station?" I
began to wonder. I stood in Lincoln Place, a badly
lit street, and without my city map I had no idea
what to do next or what direction to take. Ob-
viously I was lost again. I must have gone past
the station without noticing, or else, more likely,
after my mishap with the delivery van I'd gone
the wrong way.

Help came by chance. When I had gone a
few more steps, I noticed a pub that looked en-

ticing. I went in without a second thought and ordered a whiskey, then sat down at the heavy oak counter, beneath which ran a brass bar.

My problem was not quite as difficult as I had supposed. I traced the quadrangle of Pearse Station on a paper napkin, then added Westland Row, then the spot where I'd encountered the singing tramp; finally I reached the point where the green Ford had braked with squealing tires. I no longer had the slightest doubt: I must have gone straight past the station, then turned into Pearse Street, which ran parallel, and then gone on, as if along the third side of a triangle, all the way down to this point on Lincoln and into Kenney's Pub, for that was what the place was called.

Reassured, I ordered another drink. Following the letters of the slogan GUINNESS IS GOOD FOR YOU, my eye fell on a picture of the publican, a portrait from the belle époque, down to the last detail, the waistcoat, starched collar, moustache, and cravat. The picture's sepia tint and oval shape were reminiscent of a daguerreotype. The man had a clean-cut chin, a long, slender face, and arched eyebrows that implied a certain amazement at the world, circa 1905. The portrait hung in a dark brown frame against the walnut paneling, above rows of bottles and an electronic cash register. I thought up a task for myself: to work out how many bottles had stood on that shelf since the capture of Port Arthur, assuming that twenty bottles a week were poured down the local throats. Luckily the cash register only showed a figure of three pounds twenty-six, and I was already thinking of paying up and leaving, but as soon as I'd nodded to the barman, a familiar voice rang out in the doorway of Kenney's Pub. "Hi! We meet again!"

Then came a second, less familiar voice, saying to the first one, "Is that the Pole you bumped in the backside?"

They sat down beside me unceremoniously.

He is the eternal student, who does the odd bit of work for the left-wing press, and besides that is a writer, with two manuscripts lying at the publisher's—it's hard to break through the national mafia. She supplies *frutti di mare*, cockles, and mussels straight from the harbor to wherever they're wanted: hotels, bars, restaurants—it's a registered company.

A stream of pithy sentences flowed as I sat in the middle, happy at not having to return to my hotel yet.

"Is the Catholic empire on the retreat in your country, too?" he asked, downing his whiskey and immediately ordering another round. "The Papal tiara lording it over whole nations, go forth and multiply, multiply like rabbits! *Apropos*, has the contraceptive problem found a political solution over there in the East yet?"

"It's more of a hygiene problem," I tried to say, "especially for sailors."

But, occasionally bellowing at her—"I'm right, aren't I, Molly?"—he went on spouting words like a geyser. "Take the problem of fathers who rape their own daughters, for example! The press, our press, shocked by the confessions of little Kathleen—don't you remember what I said to you at the time, Molly?—only then did the press start beating the drum! Such rural ignorance—it makes you want to puke. All the best of them run off across the Atlantic. When you get home, you've absolutely got to write about what capitalism really means in a poor, wild Catholic country!"

He didn't want to know that I didn't write about capitalism, and when Molly reminded him of what I'd said a couple of moments earlier—where I was going—he made no effort to hide his irritation.

"It's just a pile of rubble, all that Thoor Ballylee! Rubble in the words of a poet who was nothing but a soft-brained old fool. Who did Mr. Yeats think he was? He wasn't a twentieth-century writer, that's for sure! 'Before that ruin came . . .' The old fart added his pathetic trimming. It's for old biddies and toothless Englishmen; it's like porridge, just spiced up with a bit of romantic local sauce."

"Porridge with sauce?" I asked, not quite sure if I'd understood him properly. "That's an extravagant simile."

"Leave him alone, Hugh," said Green Eyes. "He's not so stupid as to take you seriously like I do."

For a while they argued among themselves. He went on talking faster and faster, while now and then she threw in some words in Gaelic which I couldn't understand. They didn't seem to be a couple; if there was anything that did link the eternal student and the girl who sold mussels it certainly wasn't long walks along the beach at Sandy Cove, loving whispers on a bench in Phoenix Park, or hours of intoxication in a hotel room.

"I've got to go and take a leak," said Hugh suddenly. "Hold the fort, men, I've got to go and hold something else!"

He went off to the toilet humming "God Save the King" under his breath. His humming mingled with another tune, for a group of musicians, complete with guitar and violin, had sat down at the next table.

"Why do you want to go there?" asked Molly. "Are you interested in poetry?"

A couple of tomboys sat down next to the musicians; both had crewcuts, army boots, checked shirts, and leather jackets. One of the jackets bore the words AMNESTY INTERNATIONAL around a picture of a flaming candle in a ring of barbed wire.

"What interests me is a river," I said.

"What river?"

"It's called the Cloon, and it disappears not far from Thoor Ballylee."

"Disappears?"

"Yes, it goes underground. Then it flows on for another twenty miles, all the way to the Atlantic through darkness and underground rocks."

"An invisible river . . . I've never heard of that before. But I don't know much about books."

"I read about it a long time ago in a magazine called *Wonders of Nature* or something like that. You know, meteorites, magnetic rocks, and that river near a Norman tower."

"So what are the magpies chattering about now?" said Hugh, taking his seat. "Do you realize what suddenly occurred to me as I stood over the golden stream? Gogy's having a party tonight. Let's go over to his stable and see what's on show. Cause in this place," he said, indicating the tomboys, "the water soon will burst its banks and we'll wake up on Lesbos, such is her ancient name. Besides, my noble foreigner, I don't know about you, but as far as I'm concerned this is the music of Aiobhell, and the mooing of sheep's intestines has an exceptionally bad effect on one's gastric system. Perhaps you know what I mean. Oh, Gogy adores such things!" He clapped me on the shoulder. "An unexpected guest from the East! Frankincense, gold, and myrrh! Or perhaps you're a royal bastard? That would be perfect!"

"Our last king died a prisoner in Russia," I said. "Heirless. And if he did manage to beget any offspring, it was only with Catherine the Great a good many years earlier. No one knows anything about it in Moscow."

"Ha, ha, ha!" roared Hugh, delighted. "The dreaded Empress! The dreaded Kremlin! Dreadful Europe! A kingdom that doesn't exist any more!"

"Don't take any notice of him," said Molly. "It's just his style."

"The style is the man himself, once upon a time a four-legged creature, and a rather hairy one at that," said Hugh, drinking up and setting down his glass. "So, then, O progeny of the very last king and the harlot Empress, come and be a guest at Belshazzar's feast!"

Molly paid the bill. Hugh entwined his arms around us and conducted us to the exit. They were an odd pair, no doubt about it, but I was

grateful to them. The ghost of the white card was
no longer haunting me, for the time being anyway.

In the green delivery van, full of rattling empty
crates, we went down Westland Row and Pearse
Street; at Green College we turned into Grafton
Street, where Molly lived in a four-story tenement. She went in to get changed, leaving us
alone for a while. Hugh took a hip-flask from his
pocket, swigged at it heartily, and handed it to
me, saying, "Poor little thing. Do you know, her
aunt Helen was rich as a sheik but hardly left her
a penny. She was a frightful old maid, a right old
bigot, a real harridan. We went there together on
the day of the funeral. We went into the hall, and
what do you think I saw? Her bald-headed fool
of a footman giving one to the maid, on the table!
That maid—the old lady's most beloved servant
—she raked in a pretty penny. But you'll never
guess what happened to the property—the whole
lot went straight into the greedy paws of the Je-
suits! Oh, sweet Jesus! I tell you, man, that beautiful house and garden, the bank accounts, even
the silver table—the whole damned lot! All to
missions in Africa! So now the little black souls
are getting salvation for that mean old Catholic
trollop's money. But what about Molly? She
didn't even get enough cash to pay for that death-
trap car of hers—she had to get a loan from the

Allied Bank for it. What would you do with an
aunt like that?"

"I don't know," I replied. "I really don't know.
Perhaps she didn't love Molly?"

"Love?" he squealed gaily. "Love! As sounding
brass or a tinkling cymbal? Is that what you have
in mind? No, it's just a trick of the devil, my
foreign friend, ever since the serpent showed up
in the garden. Well, *sursum corda!*" he added, tip-
ping back the hip-flask. "The Greeks had a ra-
tional approach to it. Take the Judgment of Paris,
for example: the archetype of our innocence."

He took another swig, then put away the bottle
and fell silent.

Soon Molly reappeared, in a black dress, black
tights, and black ankle boots, carrying a brown
handbag. We went past Green College again, then
drove along the river and cut across a canal,
through the Irishtown district and Sandymount,
speeding westward along Merrion Road. Hugh
snored with his head tilted back, and Molly con-
centrated on the steering wheel in silence, while
I looked out at the city, which seemed completely
different by the light of street lamps, occasional
advertisements, and brightly lit house windows.

In my coat pocket I could feel the white card;
I kept turning it like a bus ticket. On the left,
against the navy blue darkness of the bay, distant
lights were glimmering, from ships, perhaps. On

the right, compact rows of buildings made space for parks and residential housing. I began to remember the evening when my father and I had got off the train at an old wooden station; in the yellow lamplight we had looked for a taxi but couldn't find one. When at last we did, the driver wasn't willing—not for any money, not for all the treasure in the world—to drive off at night to a place called Wydrwity. "You'll have to be brave," said my father. "We'll soon think of something." But we failed to think of anything; time was passing as we helplessly wandered the empty little streets around the station. We would have ended up in some hotel if it hadn't been for a cart pulled by two heavy horses. "Hey, driver, maybe you're going our way?" asked my father, a desperate question, quite devoid of any hope. Yet the peasant pulled up his team with a long drawn-out "Prrrr!" and asked what way we had in mind. "To Wydrwity," said my father. The wagoner pointed with his whip to tell us to get in, for although he was going to Sowi Rog, Wydrwity wasn't far from there, on the other side of a river and a lake.

Covered with my father's jacket, I soon fell asleep, but before that I stared into the brightness of an oil lamp. Hung on a pole, it swayed to the even rhythm like a shining pendulum, casting a circle that cut us off from the darkness into which we were sinking. When my father woke me, I saw the stars, hundreds of them in the sky. And as he pushed a borrowed dinghy out onto the water, saying, "Don't be afraid, we're not going to drown," I went on gazing at them, quite entranced. I watched their reflections in the pure black mirror of the lake, clear and silent, among rushes and reeds; I was entirely oblivious of where we were going and why, I forgot all about my father, and all about him, waiting for us over there in his hiding place at the pastor's widow's house, as if he were at the end of the world, which that corner of Ducal Prussia then was.

But now, as the van drove close to the sea and the cliffs and lighthouses flashed on and off in the darkness of the bay, I could see the sight that awaited us on the far side of the lake. It was Grandfather Karol, laid out on his back, already dead, in a white shirt with rolled-up sleeves, black trousers, and no socks, because the pastor's widow couldn't find them. I could see my father's face leaning over him to roll down the sleeves; I could see the white cloth hiding the number tattooed on my grandfather's forearm— it had three digits, one of the low Auschwitz numbers—and I could also see the scar on his chin, which was given to him by a Polish Communist, an investigating officer busy building a brave new world. There were no tears, oaths, or weeping. The pastor's widow told us it had happened when he went to bed complaining of pains in the heart. In short, dry, matter-of-fact sentences she informed us of the steps she'd taken: the death certificate lay ready on the chest of drawers, the license to transport the remains was also on display, and a man of her acquaintance from the town who had a car had already agreed to transport the body for a reasonable sum. "We're going to need a coffin," said my father. "I'll go to the city tomorrow." But the pastor's widow had seen to that as well. "The coffin is coming tomorrow, at first light," she replied. "They're bringing it here from Sowi Rog." "Why are you giving us so much help?" asked my father. "Maybe . . ." "No," she interrupted him. "Please bear in mind that there isn't much time." Those were her exact words: "Please bear in mind." Then she left us, announcing that beds were made up for us in the room he had occupied.

We had reached our destination. Hugh opened his eyes and went on with his muttered monologue on the archetype of innocence.

"This is it," said Molly. "Let's get out."

We went up a flight of stone steps that curved as they rose. Down below we could hear the crashing of the waves. Hugh, who had sobered up in no time in the cool moist air, began to spout a torrent of words again, this time about bookies at the races. I couldn't hear exactly what he was saying, and as we approached a circular building, undoubtedly once part of a fortification, I examined the rough-hewn gray blocks and wondered what kind of an eccentric would give a party here, especially since not a sound was coming from inside. Even when we were standing in front of a wooden door with a solid metal frame, it seemed as if the tower was deserted, uninhabited, and we had come to the wrong address. Inside, however, it was swarming with guests. A circular space and a steep, narrow staircase leading to the floor above were filled with a lively, babbling crowd.

My friends from Kenney's Pub forgot me.

"Hi, George!"

"Hi, Seamus!"

"Arthur, how are you?" They shouted greetings to their friends.

I didn't know a soul and felt a bit intimidated. Luckily, no one took any notice of me, so I looked around. The room reminded me of a cross between an artist's studio and a theatrical store with most of the props removed. For example, a table with bottles, glasses, and tumblers on it was like a shabby piece of furniture left over from the latter part of the eighteenth century; a chair and a chaise longue dated from the Victorian era. But there were also a number of ordinary chests, sim-

ple benches knocked together out of planks, and
even an old barrel which served as an extra little
table. Solid studs hammered into the stone walls
held up pictures or acted as pegs for the wardrobe, which was also rather theatrical. Among the
guests' coats I saw several bowler hats and top
hats hanging, and also a traveling cloak which no
court counsellor from Franz Joseph's later reign
would have been ashamed to wear. I couldn't see
anything to eat; there was nothing but bottles of
every shape and kind on the table. The guests kept
going over to it to pour themselves their chosen
drinks, so I followed suit and made my way up
the narrow staircase to the floor above.

Here, too, there was a single room, if the space
could be described as such, but with a rather
different atmosphere. Several ladies dressed in
Hellenic costume, glasses in hand, were conduct-
ing an animated conversation, apparently about
someone called Scott who was supposed to be
coming or had already arrived, an indecently rich
and handsome man. They looked as if they'd just
come off the stage or had arrived here straight
from a costume ball. Their headbands, patterned
peploses, hairdos, bracelets, and necklaces were
all in imitation of the robes of women of Delphi:
they were slender and carefree.

I went up to the second floor. Here the room
was dimly lit, and the company was discussing a

book on psychiatry and sex. One of them must have been smoking marijuana not long before— I could distinctly smell it. Maybe it was the skinny fellow in wire-rimmed glasses holding a crumpled hat, nervous, gesticulating rapidly. Or the oldish man with the look of a prewar professor. Or the vamp standing between them in a shining dress with a brocade sash and a feather in her hair.

From the ground floor to the top the tower was filled with a bizarre company, like some sort of sect or secret brotherhood. For a while I felt some regret that I wasn't one of them, but only for a while; as soon as I tried to imagine myself in a loose toga or a bowler hat, I immediately felt an urge to go on, to the uppermost floor.

I pushed open a wooden door, somewhat smaller than the one downstairs, and found myself on a round terrace encircled by battlements. The view was entrancing. I gazed out at the dark blue mantle of the bay, stretching from the rocky base of the building far, far into the distance, all the way to the dim horizon. Every now and then, at varying points in the darkness, a light flared on for a second or two, then went out, then shone again, like a twinkling star. The lighthouses were conversing with one another in their own special language, but I couldn't tell which was which or name them; my attempts to remember the map were futile. I might mistake the Poolbeg beacon for the Baily lighthouse, which stood on a rocky promontory, or for the one at the Dun Laoghaire ferry port, from which I had sailed two days earlier. It would have been easier if I'd been able to locate my own position, but even that proved unsuccessful. All I knew was that I was on the outer edge of the city, a few miles from the mouth of the Liffey.

Upstairs in the pastor's widow's house, I had looked for his work on lighthouses, but I found not even a trace of any notes. My grandfather's belongings, neatly gathered together by the widow, were limited to his clothes, shaving kit, documents, and a single old, battered, leather-bound volume. My father picked it up and in an undertone read: "Titus Lucretius Carus, De Rerum Natura." He put it down, fell silent, and hid his face in his hands. Why had my grandfather been reading a book in Latin? Why hadn't he written us any letters? Why had he been living here in seclusion, renting an upstairs room from Mrs. Nemoller? It was all terribly complicated, like the Latin book in an edition published by Brockhaus. Neither of us could sleep; we both spent the night tossing and turning in silence, both tormented by the same question—why? Was the illness that affected his mind really so severe? Or was it a sickness of the soul that had nothing to do with ordinary madness? The chirp of crickets sounded through the open window, and once in a while the mournful voice of an awakened bird came echoing from the woods.

Early in the morning the pastor's widow asked us down to breakfast. As we got up from the table, she said, straining over every word, "I've got to show it to you. He did ask me not to, but I must. I'm afraid something will have to be done with it—it really shouldn't stay here. And I haven't the strength myself."

Off we went, the pastor's widow, my father, and I, down the path across the yard, on behind the barn and into a dense crop of weeds. We walked in single file through an alder wood, across soggy ground, amid dragonflies, gnats, and green-winged insects swarming up from fern leaves and tall grass stems; lower and lower we went, along some rivulets to a point at the very edge of the lake, where a fisherman's hut made of heavy timbers stood buried in the shade of trees and rushes. "It's here," said the widow. "I won't go in there. I'm going back to the house." She turned and ran, literally leaping from clump to clump, then disappeared.

I could hear music. No, it wasn't coming from inside the hut. I was standing at the top of the

tower, and the tune was floating up from beneath
me, from one of the lower floors. A flute? A
drum? A guitar? A tambourine?

Intrigued, I went down past two floors, now
deserted. At the bottom a compact crowd stood
in a ring around the dancers—the girls I'd noticed earlier. Among them I saw a new figure—
a young man dressed as a dancer from Knossos.
He was feminine and narrow-waisted, with an
elaborate hairdo, wearing a short purple tunic
from under which showed smooth, shining, suntanned thighs.

"That's Gogy," I heard Molly whisper. "Where
on earth have you been?"

"Where's Hugh?" I whispered back.

"Oh, he got drunk again. He's somewhere on
the beach throwing up. He won't be back in a
hurry." In the air, gray with tobacco smoke and
thick with whiskey fumes, the figures of the
dancers seemed to have attained an extraordinary
lightness. "Do you like it?" she asked.

"Absolutely," I replied. "Does it symbolize
something?"

"No, it's just for fun, pure fun. When they've
finished, we're all off to the island of Meld, same
as every year. Come and sail along with us."

"The island of Meld?"

"Yes, we'll watch the sunrise from the cliffs

there. It's fantastic! Fantastic! Then we'll go to Scott's place for breakfast."

"Who is this Scott?"

"He's a millionaire, a great friend of Gogy's. And he's paying for all this."

"That's fantastic," I said.

Molly's hand touched my fingers fleetingly. But I had no desire to sail to Meld or any other island. I could feel weariness and sleep embracing my whole body. As the company began to go down toward a small pier on the beach, I asked her how to get back to the city from here.

"Come with us," she said. "It's a unique event."

"How do I get to the train from here?" I asked again.

But Molly didn't answer. Laughing, she jumped across the gangplank and was one of the last to board the motorboat, which was called *Mannan.* I didn't notice if her loquacious friend Hugh was among them. The mooring rope was cast off, and in a volley of joyful shouts the boat turned away from shore.

I set off along the beach without looking back.

"Hugh!" I cried out, "Hugh! Where are you?"

But no one answered. I passed a bathing hut marked MEN ONLY, with the message WOMEN WEL-

COME! written below. I passed some massive rocks
and heard the gentle ripple of waves washing in
between them. The tide was beginning to ebb.

I went farther, with the pungent smell of the
sea following me, and although there weren't any
sand dunes or amber, just pebbles, rocks, and
gravel, and although this was not the Baltic, it
occurred to me that Grandfather Karol might once
have set foot here, my grandfather the fireworks
seller, photographer's assistant, chemist, and
champion.

With a little luck it might have happened, but
we never did have any luck, none of us, for all
those years, as I had already realized when the
door of the fisherman's hut creaked open, and
there before our eyes that extraordinary sight appeared: amid files, saws, and drills, curved sheets
of metal and protractors, resting on iron trestles,
was the shining hull of a vessel, very like a U-
boat but smaller, clearly designed for a single person. "It's not possible . . ." my father whispered.
"It's not possible. How did he? . . . Where did
he? . . . " Carefully, tenderly, he stroked the rivets,
the hull, and the propeller, he touched the keel,
sliding his hand across the welding. "It's not
possible . . ." he whispered, bewitched by our
discovery. "He must have designed it himself, he
must have worked it all out. All on his own—

imagine getting hold of all these parts. Where on earth did he get the lathe?"

But Grandfather Karol was lying in the pastor's widow's house, unable to give an answer. We went on with our inspection of his ship, looking inside it now, ever more entranced. He hadn't forgotten a single thing. Everything about it was conceived and carried out to perfection: the double bulkheads of the ballast chambers, the conning-tower entrance, the fuel tank, the mechanism for driving the propeller by foot, quite like bicycle gears, the compartments for food, a little lamp above the map-case, a folding chair, the dashboard, spare batteries—it had everything, even a periscope with watertight casing. Under a layer of sand and sawdust, we found rails running down to the water, which was deep at that point of the shore. "Look," said my father, "the trestles have screws for wheels." Soon after that we found the wheels, and a slipway hidden in the bushes and an iron tow-chain. "If someone were to report this . . ." whispered my father. "We've got to do it quickly, understand?"

I understood. First we had to open the ballast-chamber valves, then jam the rudder, push the vehicle into the water, release it from the slipway, start the engine, and leap out of the way. It didn't take us more than a quarter of an hour. The gleaming cigar, whirring as its engine slowly turned, moved about thirty yards away from the shore, submerging ever deeper, until Grandfather Karol's wonderful creation, the fruit of his genius, disappeared with a hiss and a gurgle, vanishing forever beneath the green tract of water. We had destroyed it, or rather we'd sent it to the bottom of the lake. "Do you think . . ." I asked my father, as we were on our way back to the house. "I don't know," he replied. "That river flows out into the Vistula and it's probably pretty deep." That was all he said on the matter. He never spoke of Wydrwity again, nor of submarines, but when from time to time the radio gave a report about another Soviet submarine caught in a Norwegian fjord, he'd nervously switch it off and go into the kitchen for a smoke.

I turned away from the seashore into a small street, and proceeding on instinct alone, I finally reached a station on Summerhill Road, dazed with exhaustion. I bought a ticket from a machine and boarded the first train heading for the city. As soon as it pulled out, I fell asleep, and only a gentle prod at my arm, God knows how much later, brought me back to reality. A conductor or some sort of railway attendant—a man in uniform, anyway—stood before me, saying something I couldn't understand.

"Is this yours?" He was waving a blue rectangular object. "Did you lose this map? It was lying on the floor over there. Is it yours?"

In amazement I recognized my map of the city. There could be no doubt it was my copy, a bit ragged at the corner, with a deep crease running like a fissure across the cover.

"Yes," I said, "that's my map. But I lost it yesterday afternoon. Can that be possible?"

The man in uniform raised his cap, scratched behind his ear, and said, "Things like that do happen, but not on this line, sir." And off he went, amused.

"Which stop is this?" I called after him. "What's the next one?"

"Pearse Station," he answered, "just coming up!"

Indeed, the train was braking, and through the window I saw a sign that read PEARSE STATION. I got out and went down some steps to the exit.

Dawn was breaking. In my hand I clutched my map of the city, but I didn't stop to unfold it. I knew now that if I turned right, across the bridge, I'd get to Eden Quay, where the bus line started. If I turned left, I'd reach St. Andrew's church on Westland Row. I'd go inside and see candles, people praying, and a man with a dead list in his hand, and I'd start thinking again about Grandfather Karol. Then I'd take a card, have a chat with the priest, give a tramp fifty pence, and come within a hair's breadth of falling under a green delivery van marked LIVE COCKLES AND MUS-SELS. Did everything have to repeat itself?

So I turned neither right nor left, I went straight ahead, toward a telephone booth at the head of a rank of waiting taxis.

Back at the boarding house I slept solidly for about three hours. I took a shower, had breakfast, and went to the bus station, where I bought a ticket to Galway. I still had time before the bus left, so I drank some coffee. I reached into my pocket for a cigarette, but instead of a packet of Silk Cut I pulled out some paper and an envelope. I didn't read the form. Calmly, without reflection, I wrote crosswise over the blank lines: "My Grandfather Karol, captain of a sunken ship." I put a banknote in the envelope, kissed the card, folded it neatly, and tucked it in as well. I sealed the envelope and tossed it into a post box. As the bus was moving up the Liffey, already passing through the suburbs, and I was looking out of the window at the deep, dark green of the mead-ows, I said, "Now I'll leave you in this place, now I can go away in peace, now I know you won't come after me."

Mina

• • •

Mina had seemed somewhat unbalanced for quite a while, but the sudden eruption of her illness and its violent progression took me completely by surprise.

She came by more and more often, and would talk without pausing for two or three hours on end, chain-smoking. Her monologues first revolved around her childhood, then seamlessly drifted into the realm of her religious life, and finally, in an inevitable sequence, wandered over into the gloomy corridors of Eros.

Mina feared damnation. Her God, ever on the watch for any false step she made, any stumble or fall, was a cruel and vindictive God. He punished, but He didn't forgive. He passed judgment, but He couldn't love. He was the Creator, but He prophesied death and destruction. Mina feared this God, and in her anxiety I recognized the terror of a five-year-old girl awoken in the middle of the night to the sight of her father drunkenly hurling oaths as he beat her mother with his fists.

I was never able to convince her or make any-

thing clear to her. Her far-off childhood, in
which the monologue so often immersed itself,
as if to draw breath from it, was a distant and
unfamiliar land to me, though Mina was born
and had spent the first twenty years of her life in
the same country as I. Her small Silesian home-
town close to the German border loomed out of
her story like an exotic island. The men died
young there, usually before the age of sixty. In
the breaks between cooking and working three
shifts, the women bore children. The young men
all left the place as soon as they got the chance;
if no such opportunity came along, they drank
vodka and went down into the mines instead.
Such was the pattern of life there.

Mina also talked about her father who didn't
love her, her mother who died ten years ago, and
her brothers who had no interest in their sister's
fate. She talked about the two thousand Soviet
soldiers who were stationed in the town and
about the closed district where they lived with
their families.

Mina was immured in a terrible sensation of
cold that permeated her body.

"As if I were plunged in a well," she'd try to
explain, "as if I were falling deeper and deeper,
down where the water's freezing, where there's
not a breath of air."

She had often spent whole months on end in

this state. Even if leaves were budding outside her window or a warm June rain was falling, Mina could feel her body being wrapped in a shroud of snow, her hands turning into icicles, and a cold wind raging in her belly, her breast, and her womb.

"If only a ray of light would get through to me, if I were only to hear the word," she'd explain. "Then I'd be saved."

But HE WHOM SHE AWAITED didn't even want to look at her; he hadn't the least intention of imparting his word to her. So she gave herself to men encountered by chance, and the long-repressed flames of desire would erupt with volcanic force. However, as her body reached the heights of pleasure, her soul would be filled with anguish and anxiety. At first she couldn't explain this to herself, but in time this strange duality revealed its cause to her—she was yielding to the same man every time. The Prince of Darkness did change his appearance—he might be the swarthy man she'd met in a hotel, or the fair-haired one from the sales department—but at the moment of extreme pleasure she always recognized his features, in which beauty and ugliness combined in a most astounding way. Her shriek would pierce the air, she'd break glass if there was any at hand, or run out onto the stairway to warn people. Then the cold stage would come on, and

Mina would sink deeper and deeper into it, until the next time. HE WHOM SHE AWAITED never came, but the Prince of Darkness, his lust satisfied only for the time being, was still on the lookout for the next opportunity.

I sat and watched her tears. Mina was helpless, but my helplessness to relieve her suffering was even greater. Should we talk about God, whom Mina feared so much and who in her mind was a replica of her father? She had run away from him and the town on the German border all the way here, where she'd finished university, where, crouched for hours on end over library shelves, she earned a pittance for her keep, and where his gaze continually pursued her like an invisible force.

All her schemes, all her magic tricks to elude that gaze, which was the embodiment of power and authority, were in vain. Mina had become convinced of this several months ago when, kneeling at the confessional grille, she had done her best to explain the essence of her pain to the man in black. She told him of the flame that burst unexpectedly from beneath her dome of ice and frost; she told him of the unquenchable fires of desire that inflamed her at those moments, and of the Prince of Darkness to whom she had to submit. The man in black had dashed from the confessional and shouted words she couldn't understand, but it soon became clear—it was Him: vindictive, envious Jehovah in person. He chased her across the church, waving his arms violently and threatening her with damnation as her father had. Mina ran to the beach, where she lay on the dry sand until evening, listening to the wind blow.

"One ray of light would have been enough. One single word," she repeated, "and I would have been saved!"

In an attempt to say something, I would tell her that the ray of light or the voice she was waiting for might be very close, just a moment away, so that there was no need to despair. She would explode with rage. When two hundred angels on Mount Armon had been inflamed with desire for the daughters of the Earth, the very glance of those unearthly beings had burned the women up. Not one of them could withstand the heat, and that was the beginning of the end. Incorporeal angels, pure intelligences, joined with the dust of the Earth, for what is a woman's body if not dust? When the angels on Mount Armon joined with the dust of the Earth, that was what started the fall.

But Mina wasn't concerned with that kind of gaze, nor with the sort of light that burns and destroys. Mina was waiting for a ray of light that would touch her body tenderly and permeate her soul; to strains of music, or perhaps only to the sound of invisible breathing, it would make her blessed. HE WHOM SHE AWAITED had this kind of gaze. How could I fail to understand? How could I possibly fail to see that such very different gazes existed?

But that was about all I did see. The old mine shafts, the motionless wheels of inactive pumps, or the Russian soldiers' quarters from which the sound of gunfire or of a harmonica and singing sometimes drifted were just as far from me as the story of Mount Armon and the fallen angels. Hovering in the midst of it all, as if Mount Armon were a slag heap in Mina's little town, was the ghost of her father. This man with bushy eyebrows and hands the size of shovels had hated Mina from the day she was born in their suburban brick house.

"I was supposed to be named Helena," she explained, "but my father burst out laughing and shouted at my mother that you couldn't possibly give a name like that to such an ugly child. So he called me Mina."

The man with bushy eyebrows and hands the size of shovels craved perfection. Because the world, like Mina, their little town, and thousands of other people and towns, wasn't perfect, her father condemned it all; wherever he looked, what he saw was dusty, grimy, and full of cracks like the ones in the walls of the house they lived in before they moved to the new housing development. Mina could remember watching a bulldozer smash walls and red roof; she also remembered seeing a tree ripped out roots and all by a machine's metal jaws and left dangling against a clear blue sky for a long time afterward.

As if to spite her father, Mina grew up to be the prettiest girl in town. The men were bewitched by her breasts and her way of walking, and the Russian officers with golden epaulettes who emerged from their district now and then smelling of eau-de-Cologne and polished boot leather gazed after her with despondent faces.

"The Prince of Darkness could have been hiding in any one of them," explained Mina, "but I didn't know that yet. All I knew was that my father was waiting for my fall."

I looked at her tired face and her fingers stained yellow by cheap cigarettes. She went on spinning out her story, leaping freely across the months and years, while her inner logic was like a labyrinth with a bricked-up exit. Mina was well aware of this, and maybe that was why a look of dread lurked in her eyes. She could sense the madness enfolding her, and although she still had one foot on this side, where a lot of things could be explained without recourse to fallen angels, the other was already firmly planted over there, on the other side.

"It's as if a vortex is sucking me in," she cried, without looking up at me. "In a couple of days or so I'll latch onto the first decent guy, grab him by the sleeve, and say, 'Why don't you give me a good screw, how about it?' Or I'll stand in front of the window and throw off my clothes until someone comes and brings them to me."

She wept loudly, hiding her face in her hands. We were not really close friends. Occasionally she gave me books in the library, I'd seen her a few times in the long university corridors, and we'd exchanged a couple of remarks on the weather or the meals served in the cafeteria. I had learned that she lived alone and probably had no one to talk to. No one ever wrote letters to her or came to tea in her empty little room. Finally, after several minutes' silence, she handed me a phone number on a scrap of paper.

"Call them," she whispered. "I can't do it myself. But tell them to keep their paws off me—I'll bite them like a wild bitch. You tell them that!"

I realized it wasn't the first time she had checked herself into a hospital.

When the men in white appeared at the door, Mina calmly got up from her chair and went to their car with them. One of them quickly came back, wanting to find out more about the patient. Had she had a seizure? Might her depression be caused by conflicts with her family? Was this the first such case in the family? I said nothing. When the car drove away from my house, I breathed a deep sigh, as if I'd been relieved of a great burden.

Two days later she called me from the hospital and unloaded a whole baggage of unsettled matters on me. I was to pay her rent, go and talk to the man who ran the library, and bring her some books, her toothbrush, a towel, and her slippers from her apartment. I wasted at least half a day doing it all, and when on top of that she suggested I keep her key and water her plants for her, I put my foot down and refused. I did promise, however, that I'd come and visit her once a week.

She looked sleepy, complaining of headaches and the injections the nurses kept sticking into her. Her movements were slow and she couldn't bend her back or her neck all the way because the medicine was making her muscles stiff. In the television room where we sat and chatted other figures wandered about in their pajamas. Though the expressions on their faces were transparent and absent, I found them highly disconcerting; they seemed to be hovering around us and picking up what we were saying, as if we had something to hide. For the moment I said nothing, while Mina, her gaze fixed on the window, went on and on about HE WHOM SHE AWAITED. Why didn't he come? Was it because she wasn't worthy of such a visit? Or was it because he was disgusted by her body? He must know that apart from her body she also had a soul, and what a soul it was! How strong she felt it was, her pure, immaculate soul—he could come into it as if he were entering a crystal vase. What if he found her here in the hospital, in the middle of all these beds and the nurses' white uniforms, amid this stench and turmoil? He'd fill her up, as olive oil filling an empty jug. "He, who can place his hand in a nest of serpents, who can open all doors and locks."

A terrible shriek resounded from somewhere in the depths of the ward. I could hear shouts and people coming and going. Approaching the window, Mina went on whispering the words of her prayer more and more quietly, completely absent, lost in concentration.

One of the patients, wearing a dressing gown over his sweater, was raking a wide strip of ground by the wall. Mina appeared not to notice him. She kept talking to herself, while I observed his precise movements which looked strangely solemn from the second floor. Once in a while he broke off his work to inspect the fresh furrows he had tilled. He seemed to be looking for something, but then he shook his head in a disbelieving way and set to work again. When the nurses came to lead Mina down the corridor, the man with the rake stood motionless by the wall, staring up into the sky. Silvery clouds were gently drifting across the park, sunlight glinted idly in the leaves of the trees, and beyond the forest a passenger plane glided toward the airport.

A week later Mina's puffy face greeted me like the harbinger of bad news. She had dark rings around her eyes and a cut on her lip, and she grimaced like a witch in a children's picture book.

The bag of green apples I had brought fell across the floor. I started to pick them up, kneeling on the slippery linoleum. As if possessed by an evil spirit, she began to curse me in a low, hoarse voice. I was to blame for everything—her rage came crashing down on me with savage fury. I was the one who followed her through the university corridors and made suggestive innuendos as I returned the books I'd borrowed; I pursued her in the streets in the hope that she'd eventually give in to my impure desires, and because she hadn't, I had packed her off to the hospital where she was suffering all this torture, injections, electric shocks, and "all that shit that makes you sick."

She wouldn't let me get a word in. Again she hurled the bag of apples to the floor. Waving her arms like a robot, she hurled sexual accusations. I was the Prince of Darkness, leader of the lust-filled sons of God from Mount Armon; I was the Russian soldier who had raped her in the park just after dusk, as she was coming home from her first date; I was the doctor who had performed her abortion; it was all because of me that her father had struck her across the face, called her a bitch, and thrown her out.

I tried to get away, but Mina came after me, talking faster and faster and tugging at my arm. Streaks of saliva bubbled in the corners of her mouth, as I waited for the nurses to put an end to the scene.

Three male attendants soon came running, but with a strength I never would have suspected she had, Mina held them off for a long time.

"That's him! That's him!" she kept shouting to her tormentors, pointing at me. "He screwed little Mina! Shut the doors! Don't let him escape! Where's his uniform? Where are his golden epaulettes?"

I cannot describe how I felt at that moment. The patients and their visiting relatives were casting furtive glances at me; though they were accustomed to such scenes, I could sense a latent question in the eyes that followed me. The apples were scattered over the floor like billiard balls. I didn't stop to pick them up. As I was heading for the exit, the doctor, Professor B., a prominent figure among local psychiatrists and head of the clinic, held me back. He wanted to invite me into his office to question me about Mina, but I was already running down the stairs like one of the nurses or hospital attendants, without paying any attention to what he was saying. But he followed me, the hem of his white apron flapping in the wind, and our conversation was like an exchange of diplomatic notes, restrained and full of hidden information. Finally we stopped by a wall covered in wisteria, and I explained the nature of my friendship with Mina to him. As he was telling me about the cycles of schizophrenia, its common symptoms and baffling exceptions, I suddenly noticed the man with the rake. He was looking at the wisteria's violet flowers or at the freshly raked strip of ground that he was busy tidying, in the same way as when I had watched him from the window.

"Such a state," the professor continued, "can last for a few months. Then either the crisis passes or it doesn't. Sometimes it goes on for years." He pointed to the man stooped over the plot of earth:

"As in that man's case. Do you realize how long he's been here? Over thirty years!"

I walked down the avenue of the old park between the hospital buildings. Here and there the faces of patients looked out from behind barred windows. Only a few inmates were walking about the garden, in faded dressing gowns stamped with dark red triangles.

At the open psychotherapy ward Professor B. stopped and offered me his hand.

"Young man," he said, "it's good of you . . . it's commendable that . . . especially since our patient doesn't seem to have anyone . . ."

When I told him my name, he thought for a moment and remembered my father.

"We went sailing together on an old German hulk at the yacht club," he said, smiling broadly. "In 1946. Do you know what Gdynia looked like in those days?" As I was walking away, he said I should pay him a visit next time I came to see Mina. "Don't worry," he called after me, "she should be calmer in the future."

For the next few days I tried not to think about Mina, her illness, or the hospital.

But one night Mina came to me in a dream. She was standing on top of a brick tower: around it stretched a plain of undulating grass, and I was running toward her through thistles and teasels. In her hand she held a flaming torch, and although it was daytime, my vision was blinded by its light.

"I am not Mina, I am Helena!" she shouted when I reached her.

I awoke to find the sheets soaked with sweat.

The dream began recurring, and I could feel my own growing anxiety. I desired her body, but not the one I'd often seen in the library or the long university corridors, nor the one I could imagine in the small town on the German border. I wanted her body as it was on top of the brick tower—there it was beautiful, absolutely flawless.

Meanwhile, alarming things were happening to Mina's real body. From week to week she was growing fatter. Her puffy, bloated face reminded me of an image out of Bosch, and her total apathy and inertia further deepened the impression of remoteness, provoking a repugnance that I couldn't quite manage to stifle.

Maybe she understood what I was saying, but she only answered reluctantly, in fitful sentences. There were a lot of things I wanted to ask her about. What were her brothers doing? Was her father still alive? What had it been like with the Russian soldier in her home town that time, as she was on her way back across the deserted park at dusk, walking on wings of joy from her date when perhaps she'd exchanged her first kiss with a boy from the class ahead of hers?

But all of that remained in the realm of speculation. There was a repelling force in Mina's gaze, and none of my questions was ever even asked.

I couldn't explain why I kept going there. I had no obligations whatsoever toward Mina, and her condition was close to catatonia and worsening, shutting out communication.

My visits became shorter; I avoided meeting Professor B., but the rake man, whom I encountered every time in exactly the same spot by the wall, intrigued me more and more. He was always raking the same strip of ground, then inspecting the tracks he had made. He was clearly seeking some sign in the narrow furrows, but he would fail to find it and start raking again, stooping over his little plot. I watched his movements many times, stopping at the wall for minutes on end, but he was busy with his task and never took any notice of me.

Toward the end of summer I realized that Mina was no longer the reason I kept going to the hospital, nor was it my dream about her. It was the man in the dressing gown stamped with the letter P in a triangle, the symbol of all hospitals for the psychologically ill. His face expressed no emotion whatsoever. Never was it brightened by a smile or crossed by a look of doubt, and only as he stood stooping over his patch of earth did I notice him frowning, probably in amazement that he couldn't find whatever it was he yearned to see there. He didn't answer the timid questions I put to him once or twice: "What are you looking for? Can I help you? Have you lost something valuable?" Sometimes, at the sound of my words, he turned toward me and I got a look at his eyes. They were the same blue as Mina's, but they held a different kind of madness. His ascetic figure and Olympian calm presented a challenge. The world I had come from on the other side of the wall suddenly seemed chaotic and random, in a constant state of change, an unending stream of shapes and noises. It reminded me of a river flowing God knows where. The rake man, meanwhile, was somehow not subject to this force as he continued to perform his ritual. His eternity, which existed on a dozen or so yards of loosened soil, lay elsewhere, silent and inaccessible.

One day, perhaps the last Friday in September, they stopped bringing Mina into the visitors' room. She sat in bed, immobile, and when I looked at her face through the window of the isolation ward I realized that an invisible force, no doubt the same one that had tortured her for all this time, had cut the final thread that tied her to this world.

Behind me I heard the professor's voice, talking of somatic and hormonal changes, of the tissues, chemistry, and mysterious substances of the brain, the names of which I can't remember. He said that a hundred, maybe two hundred years from now, when biochemistry has solved these mysteries, such illnesses will no longer be incurable.

I said nothing.

The professor's voice was calm and decisive, as if he were giving a lecture to a room full of colleagues. On this side of the window the corridor resounded with "the structure of protein," "genetic mutations," and "cerebral ganglia"; on the other side sat Mina, fat, ugly, and slobbering, in a state of utter idiocy. She had to be fed, washed, dressed, and undressed like a child; she had to be cleaned from her own excrement. To all this she submitted indifferently, putting up no resistance.

Had HE WHOM SHE AWAITED come? Or had the gods of darkness, led by the angels from Mount Armon, carried off her soul and stamped their sordid seal on her body?

Could there be any other answer? I was twenty-four years old and I'd never studied theology; my Catholic upbringing hadn't prepared me at all for these kinds of questions. Yet Mina demanded an answer. Especially there, on the far side of the window, where she was utterly helpless and desolate.

Meanwhile the professor went on talking; it was some time before I realized he was telling me the story of the rake man. In the days when an ammunition truck drove down the beach every evening, the man had been a border guard. Every morning at daybreak he had patrolled his stretch of the route, and every morning, he was later to claim during hours of interrogation, he found the tracks of bare feet leading from the sand dunes to the sea. He didn't report it to his superiors. If the footprints had led in the opposite direction, he might have assumed, in accordance with his orders, that a spy had emerged from a submarine. But why barefoot, and why in exactly the same place every day? He couldn't answer these questions any more than he could explain why the footprints always led to a point where the waves washed them away. He spent night after night on watch, hoping for an explanation of the mystery. He never saw a soul, but the footprints were always there, as if someone was making fun of the border guards. The footprints wouldn't let him rest; they became his obsession and his curse. Whatever he did, he couldn't free himself of the thought that the next morning, marching along the wide strip of plowed beach with his gun slung over his shoulder, he would find the tracks of those bare feet in the same spot. He followed them to the sand dunes, but the trail broke off

there, as if someone had materialized out of thin
air with the sole purpose of crossing the sandy
hill, cutting across the plowed strip, and then
vanishing into the sea.

I wondered why the professor was telling me
this story. When I was sitting in his office, drinking tea from a china mug, the reason became
clear.

"Those footprints," he said, adjusting his
horn-rimmed glasses, "were never actually there.
He must have already been suffering from certain
disorders which, if they had been discovered in
time, might not have led to tragedy."

It had happened in 1951, at daybreak, as the
mist was settling and the first rays of sunlight
were shining on the sea. Lying in wait, as he had
done for many nights, the guard dozed off. When
he was awoken by the daylight, his heart shuddered. A figure was approaching from the sand
dunes, moving lightly across the plowed beach,
barely touching the ground. The guard, who
couldn't tear his eyes from it, claimed afterward
over and over that two large wings were sprouting from its back. "Stop or I'll fire!" he had
shouted, but the figure—he couldn't see whether
it was a man or a woman—took no notice of his
shouts; it kept moving along the shore. He
squeezed the trigger once, twice, aiming slightly
above the shoulder blades, between the wings.

When he ran to the shore, he found a young girl of nineteen or twenty, lying motionless, staring up at the sky. The waves lapped at her bare feet, and dark blood was rapidly soaking into the sand. She was dead, but he couldn't see the wings anywhere. That's how they were found an hour later—she lying with her feet in the water, he kneeling beside her weeping, touching her cheeks, and stroking her long hair.

"They never did manage to establish the girl's identity," continued the professor, "and to close the matter they recorded it as an attempted illegal border crossing. The guard was transferred to barracks so he wouldn't have to walk up and down the beach any more, but a couple of months later it came to light that he was quite simply mad. 'I killed an angel,' he wrote in a succession of reports to his superiors, 'and may God send punishment down on me and on this whole accursed country where such crimes are allowed to happen.' That's when he was sent here," said the professor, lighting a cigarette. "In those days I was just an assistant and I was present at his examination. He couldn't explain why no one else had seen the footprints in the sand, and he claimed the wings must have flown to heaven on their own, because God would never have allowed them to fall into the hands of mortals."

Soon after that the man had asked for a rake

and had started his daily ritual of tending the patch of earth by the wall.

"Thirty years," said the professor, after a brief silence. "That's how much time has passed since he first asked for the rake. There was a journalist who was interested in his story," he went on, "you know the kind of thing . . . digging up the past, investigating that era. But he never managed to find the grave of the girl who was supposed to be an angel. He never even got hold of the records of the case. As for him," said the professor, pointing out of the window, "he doesn't say a word. Since he began raking his plot by the wall, he has stopped talking. There won't ever be any newspaper coverage; who in their right mind would believe such a story?" The professor gave a short, dry laugh.

As we were walking through the park to the hospital gates, he told me that Mina might remain in a state of stupor for as long as the rake man or even longer. He explained what complex processes occur in the brain and throughout the nervous system, processes we cannot define let alone control, but I was thinking about the handle of the rake. It was smooth and shiny like the wood of church pews, handled in exactly the same place over and over.

"Sometimes," the professor ended his account, "all it takes is a slight change in the chemical composition of the tissue or the fluid, and we start seeing angels and devils, we start hearing voices, and you never know how it'll end. Please do give me a ring some time, but there's really no reason to come here again for now," he said.

Indeed, there was no reason to go there again. Mina would never get any better. No miracle occurred to restore her health and her former appearance, nor has any biochemical substance been discovered that might cure her.

Eight years have passed since then. I know that Mina, shut away in a special ward, has an attack of frenzy a couple of times a year, followed by a period of total apathy and passivity.

I often think of her, and every time I do, I remember my final visit to the hospital, the last time I ever saw her. This was two months after my conversation with the professor. The trees in the park had lost their leaves, and half-frozen puddles crunched beneath my feet. The nurse who was escorting Mina straightened her coat, which had been thrown on over her dressing gown. Mina stopped and stood by the wall. Someone inside the building started calling to the nurse from a window. The nurse hesitated for a moment, but since I was standing nearby, he left Mina and ran inside. Then something strange happened: the rake man, wearing a wool hat and a ragged old sheepskin coat, lay down his tools, fell to his knees, folded his hands as if at worship, and began to whisper a prayer to Mina. She stood there on the freshly raked plot. The wind was blowing dry leaves off the wall, and the first flakes of snow swirled in the air, settling on her hair like a silvery net. They looked into each other's eyes, he praying to her, and she receiving his words in silence. When the nurse returned to take Mina by the arm and lead her back to the ward, it occurred to me that both of them had been waiting a long time for this meeting by the wall, and that both of them were very happy at that moment, if happiness means a temporary relief from suffering, a pause in which our piercing pain is no longer felt.